D0431594

NEWHAM LIBRARIES

90800100264441

A MESSAGE FROM CHICKEN HOUSE

I've always loved jungle thrillers – here, the forest becomes a character of its own, dangerous and wild. The sense of threat is heightened in *Boy X* as frightening animals prowl in the corners of your eyes, flitting between the trees . . . The mystery and excitement are pitch-perfect and, like Dan's readers everywhere, I feel it's me caught up in the adventure, trying to outguess the twists and turns in the plot. Get ready to be excited and intrigued!

BARRY CUNNINGHAM
Publisher
Chicken House

BOY X

DAN SMITH

Chicken House

2 Palmer Street, Frome, Somerset BA11 1DS
www.chickenhousebooks.com

Text © Dan Smith 2016

First published in Great Britain in 2016
The Chicken House
2 Palmer Street
Frome, Somerset BA11 1DS
United Kingdom
www.chickenhousebooks.com

Dan Smith has asserted his right under the Copyright, Designs and
Patents Act 1988, to be identified as the author of this work.

All rights reserved.
No part of this publication may be reproduced or transmitted or utilized
in any form or by any means, electronic, mechanical, photocopying
or otherwise, without the prior permission of the publisher.

Cover and interior design by Steve Wells
Typeset by Dorchester Typesetting Group Ltd
Printed and bound in Great Britain by CPI Group (UK) Ltd, Croydon CR0 4YY

The paper used in this Chicken House book is made from wood
grown in sustainable forests.

1 3 5 7 9 10 8 6 4 2

British Library Cataloguing in Publication data available.

PB ISBN 978-1-909489-04-2
eISBN 978-1-910655-52-8

This is for you.
You are stronger than you think you are.

Also by Dan Smith

My Friend the Enemy
My Brother's Secret
Big Game

Light.

Bright. White. Light.

Ash's eyes snapped open, bringing intense pain, making him close them again and put his hands up for protection. A sharp ache bored through his skull and he lay still, trying to remember where he was.

For a moment his mind was blank, then his stomach heaved as an image leapt into his head. He had been at Dad's funeral – all those black suits and sad faces. People he hardly knew, talking about what a good bloke Ben McCarthy had been. There was something else, though. There had been something *wrong*. Something to do with that scruffy pot-bellied man. Whatever he'd said to Mum had sent her into a panic and she had dragged Ash away, and . . .

And now he was here, in this firm bed, beneath crisp, clean sheets.

As soon as the pain started to ease, Ash pushed himself up on his elbows and squinted at the unfamiliar room. The ache of panic stirred deep inside like an awakening beast.

As everything came into focus, he saw that the room was bare. White walls reflected light from a fluorescent tube set behind a frosted glass panel in the white ceiling. Attached to the wall on the right-hand side of the bed was a panel with three touchscreens displaying digital numbers in glowing orange and green. A clear tube sprouted from the centre of the panel, running down to a blue plastic connection that was stuck to the back of Ash's right hand by a large piece of clear tape. Beneath the tape, the needle that entered his skin was just visible. The sight of the shining steel piercing his body sickened him. For some reason it made him think of spiders in the dark.

'Mum?' His throat was dry and his voice croaked. His mouth felt as if it were filled with cotton wool, soaking up every last drop of moisture.

On a small bedside table was a plastic cup, and next to that was Dad's identity disc. The leather cord was coiled like a small black snake. Ash looked at the disc for a moment, trying to remember what had happened. His thoughts were muddled though, prodding the panic-beast harder, so he kept his eyes fixed on the identity disc; the one thing that could make him feel strong.

He reached out and took hold of the leather cord that uncoiled as he lifted it. The tag swung from side to side and he sat up further, using both hands to slip it over his neck. It was the only familiar thing in an unfamiliar room, and having it lying against his chest made him feel safer.

When that was done, he took the cup, drank half the water, then replaced it on the table and swung his legs over the side of the bed. The floor was white, with faint flecks of green running through it. It was cold on his bare feet.

He felt even smaller than usual as he sat there and looked around the room, trying to remember everything that had happened since the—

He injected you, said the voice in his head.

It was the same voice Ash had heard all his life. It had always been there to taunt him and doubt him; to make him feel useless and afraid.

Don't you remember that little syringe? He drugged you. A slender man without any expression and a smooth, deep voice. And now you're dead. All alone.

The voice made his stomach queasy, so Ash touched the identity tag for reassurance and glanced down to see he was wearing pale blue, light cotton pyjamas. He felt an uncomfortable flush of anger and embarrassment; some-one else must have put them on him. Maybe he was in some kind of hospital or something. That would explain the white sheets and white walls.

'Mum?' His voice was flat in the small white room, and panic tightened its grip. He waited a few seconds, then called again, this time louder. 'Mum?'

Nothing.

She died, sneered the voice in his head. It came from somewhere dark and out of reach. *They stuck a needle in her neck and she got what she deserved. She's dead and gone and you're all alone.*

'No.'

It wasn't true. He would know, wouldn't he? He would feel it.

Ash pushed to his feet and put a hand on the wall to steady himself. Without even thinking about it, his fingers went to the tag round his neck, and a hollow ache nestled among all the other terrible feelings. He shook it away and looked down at the needle in his hand. If he were going to leave this room, search for Mum, he would have to remove it.

'I *have* to.' He peeled back the tape and the needle fell to one side, almost sliding out by itself. Clear liquid oozed like venom from the tip as he dropped the needle onto the bed and rubbed the back of his hand.

The numbers on the digital panel began to change and Ash was afraid something terrible was about to happen. Maybe the drip was keeping him alive and now his brain would cloud over, or his heart would stop beating, and—

There was no change at all. Nothing.

Ash stayed where he was for a few more moments, staring at the numbers, then turned towards the door set into the far corner of the room. Taking a deep breath, he padded over to it.

It'll be locked.

He knew it straight away, as surely as he knew his name was Ash McCarthy and that in three weeks' time he would be thirteen years old. Whoever had brought him here would have locked the door.

Preparing for the worst, he reached out and took the handle firmly in his hand, then twisted and pulled.

The overhead door-closer made a sucking noise as it opened, and Ash stepped back in surprise. The voice had been wrong. With his fingers still on the handle, he listened, hardly daring to cross the threshold. He wanted to know where he was and what was out there, but at the same time he *didn't* want to know.

His fingers curled harder round the handle and his stomach cramped as if the panic-beast had breathed ice. He was tempted to call out, but something told him it was better to be quiet and unnoticed, so he took a step, leaning forward just enough to peek out.

The corridor ran in both directions. Long and white, with the same green-flecked floor. It was silent and empty. No nurses or doctors hurrying here and there carrying clipboards and clicking pens. No trolleys, or visitors.

Just a long, white, empty corridor, and the steady hum of air conditioning.

See? You're already dead. You're in hell.

The corridor was lined with doors on both sides, spaced evenly. Each one had a Roman numeral on it, close to the top. He turned and looked at his own door, seeing a little, black, plastic 'X'.

Without warning, another flash of memory sparked in his

mind – of a woman injecting his mum the same way the man had injected him. And the woman had said something.

Kronos needs to be resurrected.

Ash didn't know what that meant, but he remembered the look on Mum's face.

It had filled her with terror.

Ash wanted more than anything to be safe and warm; to slip back into the room, push the cupboard across the door and climb into bed. But he had to find Mum.

He stepped into the corridor and the door-closer made that strange, airy sucking noise as it swung shut behind him.

Ash had never felt so small and alone. His only protection was a pair of flimsy pyjamas, and his soft, bare feet padded on the vinyl floor, sticking with each step, reminding him how vulnerable he was.

Pad-shtik. Pad-shtik.

When he reached the next door along the corridor, he stopped and stood for a long time, shivering.

A strange smell settled in his nostrils; not the smell of hospitals or dental surgeries, but something else. At first, it was as if the air was dead, but when he breathed deeper, filling his lungs, he tasted the odd tang of metal. There was plastic and paint, cleaning fluids, oil, chemicals and . . .

Smells flooded into him, overwhelming him.

His head spun and he put out a hand to support himself against the doorframe. He had never experienced such a powerful rush of odours. They slammed into him as if someone was raining punches on him. He put his free hand to the tag round his neck and spoke under his breath. 'I am Ash McCarthy. I am strong. I can do this.'

Whenever they went on one of Dad's days out, trying to get Ash to do something that scared him, Dad said it didn't matter how difficult or scary things were, if you could stay positive and be confident you could overcome anything. He told Ash that it helped to have some words to give you strength. He called it 'the McCarthy Mantra', even though Ash wasn't exactly sure what that meant.

'I am Ash McCarthy. I am strong. I can do this.' He repeated the words over and over, picturing each one in his mind, using them to push away the overpowering mixture of smells. And as they began to fade, one smell remained, heightened above all the others. Perfume. Mum!

Mum might be in there. She might be in danger. Ash gripped the door handle and turned until it clicked, then crept into the room, but there was nothing to see other than a bed, a cupboard and a bedside table. Just like his own room.

There was *something*, though. The smell of Mum's perfume grew stronger as he approached the bed, as if someone were holding the bottle right under his nose. It was so *clear*. There was something else too, something even harder to explain. When he stood beside the bed, looking down at the disturbed sheets, Ash could smell his mum. It made him think of shampoo and shower gel, fresh air and, of course, that perfume. Ash could pick out each odour – it was the strangest sensation, but what really mattered was that Mum had been here. There were even a few strands of her dark hair on the white pillowcase.

In that moment, Ash felt so close to her and yet so far away and so helpless that the panic-beast almost became uncontrollable inside him. He wanted to collapse onto the bed and put his head in his hands and let the tears come, but he crushed that feeling down inside him; told himself not to be so pathetic. Maybe Mum needed his help. What use would he be to her if he just sat there and cried?

Crushing his fear into a hardened nugget and pressing it deep inside, Ash slipped back into the corridor and continued searching, Mum's scent fading until there was no sign she had ever been there.

Pad-shtick. Pad-shtick.

Ash tried every door, checking each identical room, but found all of them empty and unused. When he finally reached the end of the corridor, he peered through the narrow glass panels on either side of the exit, and into another corridor beyond. It ran perpendicular to this one, making a 'T' shape, disappearing in both directions.

Immediately in front of him, on the other side of the glass, was a wide set of stairs heading down.

After hesitating for just a moment, Ash pushed through the exit and darted across. At least now he was going somewhere. Ten steps down, there was a small landing and the staircase came back on itself. Ash descended further into what looked like the lobby of some kind of office building.

Inside the enormous domed space, he was surrounded by tinted glass that reached high overhead. And right in the centre of the tiled floor below it was a large, round reception area, like an island: a waist-high wall of dark wood polished to a brilliant shine. Just behind it, standing on a slab of similar coloured wood, were a number of imposing stainless-steel letters, each of them at least one metre high. They spelt a single word:

BI✸MESA

The letter 'O' was made to look like a black sun with eight rays radiating from it, but Ash thought it looked like a fat spider with short legs. He had always thought that, for as long as he had known the logo; it was the name of the company his mum worked for.

See? It's her fault, the voice said. *This is all her fault.*

What was her fault? None of this made any sense. Mum had a boring job. She was some kind of researcher at the pharmaceutical place outside town.

Ash ran his hand along the surface of the counter,

breathing in the scent of wax and leather. The acrid tang of electricity. The different odours were vibrant and individual but didn't overwhelm him like before. It was strange that each smell was so clear – as if they were enhanced.

He passed an entrance cut into the back of the reception area, like an old-fashioned shop counter, and saw that within this circular island of wood four empty chairs stood behind four computers with blank screens. Everything was switched off and there were no papers on any of the surfaces. No pens or paperclips or photographs. It looked unused.

But that wasn't what demanded his attention. It was what he saw through the tinted glass that surprised Ash the most. He wasn't in England any more, that was for sure.

'Where the *hell* am I?'

Beyond the front door Ash could see a large clearing surrounded by a fifteen-metre tall chain-link fence. On the other side of it, there was nothing but trees. But they weren't oak and sycamore and horse chestnut. They weren't the kind of trees that lined the grey, rain-soaked street he lived on.

These trees were thick and green and leafy. They grew close together and were topped with fronds and fans. Some had strange, grotesque roots, some had trunks spiked like medieval weapons, while others were fat, with contorted faces hidden in knotted bark. They sprouted unfamiliar fruits, and many were hanging with vines.

Ash couldn't believe what he was seeing. It looked like

jungle, and even through the tinted glass of the dome he could tell it was bright out there, because light glittered among the leaves like jewels, and in the centre of the clearing a large, black helicopter gleamed in the sun. Almost without thinking, he crossed the lobby and padded towards the exit.

As he came closer, the sensors detected him and the doors swished open, letting in a blast of hot, humid air. It took his breath away, rushing down into his lungs and making him gasp, bombarding him with a sensory overload. The world was *alive* out there.

Ash put his hands to his ears and closed his eyes as the powerful jumble of sights, sounds and smells flooded his senses. It was like a TV on full volume, flicking from channel to channel, never pausing on anything for more than a split second. Everything was amplified, as if someone had turned all the dials up to eleven inside his head. There was a continuous chirping of insects, the bright and cheerful call of birds, the rustle of the breeze in the treetops. Ash could hear the hum of electricity from the chain-link fence – a high-pitched, irritating whine that veiled everything like a thin cotton sheet. And after all that white inside the building, colours exploded in his vision – a million different shades of green, splashes of red, snatches of yellow and purple and pink. There was the scent of dark earth too, the strong perfume of flowers and the cloying stink of helicopter fuel.

In blind confusion, he dropped to his knees and curled into a tight ball, trying to clear his mind. He had to make it go away. He opened his mouth to scream, but a single image jumped into his head.

Dad.

Dad was telling him not to be afraid. That he was strong.

'I *am* strong,' Ash whispered to himself. 'I *can* do this.'

He focused on those words, and instead of trying to push the smells away, he accepted them. Instead of trying to shut out the sounds, he took his hands away from his ears and let himself hear them. And when he eased open his eyes, he allowed the colours to flood in.

He reached again for the tag round his neck and squeezed it between finger and thumb. 'I *am* strong,' he said, louder now, daring to look around. 'I am *strong*.'

The sounds and smells and sights began to settle. He found that he could control it better, choose the things he wanted to hear, although there was still that high-pitched whining that made his stomach queasy.

Ash scanned the forest. Everything was so clear. He could see each individual leaf on the trees beyond the fence. He could spot the movement of the birds in the branches. It was as if he had spent the past thirteen years looking at the world through a greasy window that had just been cleaned. And now that he had accepted the sounds, he could pick out the song of each individual bird.

It was confusing. Frightening. Amazing.

He got up and moved out into the clearing as if it were a new world. The heat wrapped around him like a comfortable blanket. The doors swished closed behind him as he walked onto the wide-bladed grass, warm and spongy under his bare feet. He approached the helicopter that sat like a sleek animal, reaching out to touch it, wondering if he had travelled here on it. The paintwork was blistering hot and he snatched his fingers away, thinking it must have been sitting there a while beneath the intense sun.

How long had he been asleep? How long had he been in this place?

Once again, Ash looked at the solid wall of jungle beyond the fence, no more than a hundred metres in front of him. He remembered when he had visited Mum's family in Trivandrum, and Dad had taken him into the forest a few times. He'd wanted to show Ash different ways to make a fire and how to build a shelter, and they had even spent a whole night in there, surrounded by the intense darkness and the terrifying noises. Ash hadn't got much sleep, but Dad had been pleased with him – told him he'd make a good jungle survivor one day.

Ash hadn't been so sure; sleeping in a comfortable bed was much better than an unstable hammock under a leaky poncho. Roasting chunks of Mum's tandoori chicken over the fire had been good, though, and at least the mosquitoes had left him alone, even though they'd feasted on Dad.

Ash wondered if maybe that's where he was now. India. Maybe this *was* all something to do with Mum.

He saw that the building he had come from was a large, concrete dome-like structure with the glazed lobby area protruding like the entrance to an igloo. The glass was mirrored on the outside and the sun blazed from every surface of it. Trees curved around the whole area, following the line of the fence as if the building was inside a massive clearing. And Ash didn't like the look of that fence. The way it hummed with electricity made him shiver when he realized it must be there to keep something in.

Or to keep something out.

Over to his right, he spotted a gap in the fence. It was difficult to tell from this angle, but there appeared to be a fenced-off path leading into the jungle, which—

A noise.

It was faint, but unmistakeable: footsteps.

Ash froze, unsure what to do, and a moment later a pair of startled birds rose from the trees. With black and white markings like a magpie, they squawked and clattered their wings as they flew high and separated, disappearing over the forest. Ash wondered how he could have heard the noise before the birds.

The footsteps came closer, and he saw movement through the links in the fence. His instinct was to get away from whoever was coming. But this was the first sign of life he had seen since waking. Maybe they could help him.

Maybe it was Mum.

A figure came along the path and emerged through the gap into the clearing. She moved into the open, swinging a stick, and walked a few metres before catching sight of Ash and halting in her tracks.

The girl was young, maybe about his own age, with olive skin and long dark hair parted down the middle. It occurred to Ash that she might be dangerous and want to hurt him – or bring other people who would hurt him. Adrenalin was firing through his blood, making his whole body tingle, preparing it for whatever was coming next. His eyes flicked from the girl to the ground as he searched for a rock, a stick, any kind of weapon.

The girl pulled her left hand from the pocket of her combat trousers and raised it in greeting. '*¡Hola!*' she called out. '*¿Cómo estás?*'

Ash was still half turned, ready to run, and his fists were balled, ready to fight.

'*¡Hola!*' she said again with a wave. 'Hello.'

It looked and sounded like a friendly greeting. '*¿Te has perdido?*' she asked. 'Are you lost?' She swung the stick up and rested it on her shoulder before heading towards Ash, bringing with her the sweet smell of ginger and cinnamon. A hint of coconut too. 'Speak English?'

He nodded.

'You must be from the helicopter.' She had a thick accent, as if English wasn't her first language. 'You looked . . . how you say? Out of it.'

As she came closer, Ash stepped back, holding up his fists.

The girl stopped. She glanced at the stick in her hand, then frowned and threw it to one side. 'I won't hurt you.'

Ash kept his guard up.

'My name is Isabel.' She pronounced it *Ee-sa-bell*.

Confused and still wary of her, Ash remained silent and suspicious. He looked the girl up and down, seeing her jungle boots, T-shirt and combat trousers. He wondered what she must think of him — a skinny boy, shorter than average, wearing nothing but a pair of pyjamas.

When Ash didn't answer, the girl shrugged. 'I like your hair. It looks cool. The white.' She put a finger to her head and drew it from front to back. 'It looks good.'

Ash narrowed his eyes. 'Where are we?'

'*Isla Negra*.' She flicked her head to sweep away a strand of hair that had fallen across her eyes. 'Black Island. And that is the BioSphere.' She gestured towards the building.

Ash didn't like the sound of 'Black Island', or 'the BioSphere', but all he could do was add them to the list of things he didn't like about this place. 'You saw us arrive? My mum too?'

'*Sí*. Two days ago.'

It was like a slap in the face. *Two days*? How was that possible? Surely Ash couldn't have been asleep for two days. 'Do . . . do you know where my mum is?'

Isabel touched the collar of her faded black T-shirt. 'In the . . .' She paused. 'In the lab-or-a-tory, I guess.' She nodded once, pleased to have got the word right. 'With Papa.'

'You've seen her?' Ash felt a glimmer of relief. 'She's all right?'

'Your mama is . . . *morena* like you? Brown skin? With dark hair like mine? About this high?' She held her hand about thirty centimetres above her head.

'Yeah.'

'Then I did see her. She came off the helicopter with you and the others. I asked Papa who you are, but he said it is a secret. There are many secrets here, so I don't ask again.

Come. I take you to Papa.' With that, Isabel walked past, heading towards the BioSphere.

Ash hesitated, afraid to trust her.

'Come,' Isabel insisted, and smiled at him. 'We'll find your mama.'

There wasn't much choice, so Ash followed, asking, 'What is this place? Where is everyone?'

The doors swished open and they walked into the cool interior of the building.

'I already told you. *Isla Negra,*' Isabel said. 'It is an island near Costa Rica.'

'*What?*' Ash couldn't hide his shock. 'Costa Rica? Isn't that, like, South America or something?'

'*Central* America. And we are not many here. Just a few, until you came to—'

Her last words were interrupted by the loudest and most awful wailing. A high-pitched electronic screeching that drilled into their heads.

Isabel stopped with her mouth open and put her hands to her ears, but Ash hunched, stunned by the outburst. It felt like an enormous spike was being hammered through his skull, and he screamed in pain.

He squeezed the identity tag tight in his fist and imagined he was back at home in his bedroom with his headphones on, listening to music. Mum and Dad were downstairs and everything was as it should be. Everything was *normal*. After a few seconds, the pain began to fade and the sound withdrew as if being dragged away along a tunnel. The harder he concentrated, the easier it became.

'Are you OK?' Isabel was shouting in his ear. 'Are you—'

'Yes.' Ash let go of the tag and held up his hand. 'I'm . . . I'm fine. What's that noise? He opened his eyes and looked at her.

'The alarm,' Isabel said. 'Something must have happened.'

Then, from somewhere inside the building came a sound that was far more frightening. Ash had never heard it before in real life, but he had seen enough films and played enough video games to know what it was.

Gunfire.

They were still standing there in shock when the alarm cut out. Ash's ears were ringing, and it felt like someone had been slapping him round the head.

'What's going on?' he asked. 'I have to find—' He stopped. 'Wait. Someone's coming.'

'I don't hear anything.'

But Ash could hear it as if it were right beside him. The sound of running. He turned as two men came into view, hurrying down the stairs at the far end of the lobby.

The first man jumped the last few steps and hit the tiled floor with a *thump*! He landed in an awkward position, twisting his ankle and falling to his knees. He swore and struggled to his feet as the second man grabbed his arm to pull him up. As soon as they started moving again, the first man hobbling on one leg, they spotted Ash and Isabel.

Brrratatat! From somewhere upstairs came another short burst of gunfire.

'Get out of here!' the first man shouted as they hurried past. 'It's not safe. Not for anyone. Come with us.'

Ash stepped back as the doors swished open. 'We can't. We have to find my mum.'

'My papa works in there too.' Isabel watched the men leave the building and make straight for the helicopter. When they reached it, the one with the twisted ankle pulled open the door and climbed in.

Brrratatat!

This time the shots were much closer, as if right above them. And then came the sound of pounding footsteps echoing down the stairwell.

'Hide.' Ash darted away from the staircase, towards the wooden reception area in the centre of the lobby. Isabel hesitated, then followed as Ash skidded under the fold-down section and slipped beneath the lip of the counter, right below the computers.

Seconds later came the thunder of several pairs of boots on the steps.

'There they are!' It was a woman's voice; commanding and strong. 'Stop them!'

For one terrifying moment, Ash thought she had seen *them*; that she was sending someone after *them*. But then she shouted, 'Don't let them take off!' Boots pounded on the lobby tiles, racing straight past them and fading as the doors swished open and people hurried outside.

Ash looked into Isabel's dark brown eyes, seeing that she was just as scared and confused as he was. 'We're going to be all right.' He said it as much for himself as for her.

'Why are they doing this?' Isabel whispered. 'Why are they shooting?'

'I'm going to look.'

'No.'

'I have to see.' With a deep breath, Ash stood just enough so that his eyes were above the counter, and he peered through the glass at what was happening outside.

As soon as he spotted the woman, a memory blind-sided him. It came out of nowhere like a speeding car and slammed into him with great force. *You remember her*, said the voice. *She came to your house. Called herself 'Cain'.*

Ash's thoughts swum as if he'd just woken from a dream; images coming back to him. He had been in his room, looking out of the window when he had seen the shiny black Range Rover speeding down his cul-de-sac. Gleaming black alloys and smoked-out windows, it had stopped outside his house, and a man and woman had come to the door. When Mum had answered it, they'd pushed their way in and—

Injected you. Brought you here.

Ash shook the voice away and stared at the woman called Cain. Athletic and confident, she wore camouflaged combat trousers and jacket, with a dark green vest covered in bulging pockets. Her black hair was pulled back in a ponytail, and she had a cap on her head, the peak bent into a curve. She was wearing black military boots and carried a short assault rifle. Ash recognized it from the video games he had played. It was an M4 carbine, and right now, the woman was standing in front of the helicopter, pointing it directly at the glass cockpit.

There was a man with her, armed and dressed the same, as if it were some kind of uniform. He was huge, like the Hulk, with broad shoulders and almost no neck. He was trying to pull open the helicopter door while Cain was shouting something, and Ash turned his ear towards it, trying to hear as he had heard before, but the glass was too thick and he couldn't make out anything more than a mumbling. From her tone he guessed Cain was ordering the men to get out of the helicopter. It didn't look as if they were going to do what she said, though, because the helicopter engines roared into life and the rotor blades began to move.

'They're leaving?' Isabel said.

Cain turned her head as if she had heard. She looked across at the building and her cold blue eyes met Ash's.

'Get down!' He ducked.

As soon as he was below the counter, Ash started to shuffle under, his throat burning from the acid that had risen from his stomach. Cain had seen him, and now she was going to—

Mirrored glass.

Cain couldn't have seen him because it was impossible to see into the building from outside. The glass was smoky from the inside but mirrored from the outside.

Ash told himself to calm down, and rose up for another look.

Cain was still turned in his direction. She had a finger to her ear, and was speaking as if arguing with someone.

The helicopter engines were whining, audible even inside the lobby, and the rotor blades were gathering speed. Cain's cap peeled back and whipped away in the draught but she ignored it and continued speaking. After a few more seconds of animated conversation, she nodded and turned back to the helicopter.

She lifted her weapon and aimed directly at the cockpit.

Hulk realized what she was about to do and jumped away from the door.

Brrratatat!

Ash heard the muffled gunfire as the weapon kicked in Cain's hands and the cockpit glass shattered, but she was too late. Already the aircraft was leaving the ground and the skids were a few metres above the grass.

'Bring it down!' A voice came from the stairwell behind them. 'You can't let them leave!'

Ash and Isabel ducked back under the counter as footsteps echoed down and past them, then there was a roar as the doors swished open and the amplified sound of the helicopter flooded into the lobby.

Ash risked poking his head up again, and saw a pot-bellied man in a dishevelled suit stride out and look up at the rising helicopter. He was older than the others, short and scruffy, with messy hair. He wore dark-rimmed glasses and had a close-clipped beard. Over his shoulder was a zipped-up messenger bag.

The man from the funeral! The same one who had sent Mum into a panic.

Following just behind him was an athletic man with bright orange hair, and then came two more soldiers carrying a wooden crate between them. It was the kind of thing used for transporting animals, with poles slipped through loops of rope on each side so they could carry it more easily – one from the front and one from behind. There were six rows of small air holes in the side of the crate, and two large round ones on the front, covered with a metal mesh. For one horrifying moment, Ash wondered if his mum might be in there.

As the doors closed behind them, the man in the scruffy suit pointed at the aircraft and yelled something at Cain.

Cain looked round at Hulk, then they both raised their weapons and began firing.

Brrratatat!

Bullets thumped into the helicopter, punching holes right along the underside as it rose high above the trees. On the ground, Cain ejected her spent magazine and pulled another from a pocket in her vest, reloading and firing again.

The untidy man from the funeral stood back against the glass lobby as the aircraft rose and slipped sideways like an animal trying to escape the irritating prattle of the bullets. When it was way above the trees, the nose dipped and it looked for a second as if it might actually escape. But then the machine twisted and the tail dropped, lifting the nose so it was pointing at the sky.

Cain and Hulk continued to fire as the helicopter tipped further back, then jerked to the left and began to drop.

It came down hard and fast.

Cain and the others stopped shooting and ran towards the building to escape the crashing aircraft. As they came, the door opened, letting in the sound of the struggling engine. Whatever was in the crate must have been important because the two men didn't put it down. Despite the extra weight, they ran with it back to the BioSphere, followed by their orange-haired colleague.

At the far edge of the clearing, the helicopter's rotors clipped the forest canopy, jolting the aircraft into a lazy spin that twisted it first one way, then the other, as it whirled towards the ground, hitting the grass with a sickening crunch.

Even then, the helicopter continued to spin, flicking round as if it were nothing more than a toy. The tail boom smashed into the electric fence, sending up a shower of sparks. It tore through the mesh and hit the base of a large tree. There was a sharp scream of metal as the tail tore off, then what was left of the aircraft flipped over onto its side, the rotors ripping away and breaking into pieces that shot across the clearing like missiles.

Plumes of dust and smoke rose from the crash site, billowing across the ground, rising to form a huge cloud that washed over the clearing. It rolled towards Ash and Isabel like a tidal wave, forcing its way through the open doors. It smashed into the lobby, spraying everything with soil and broken twigs, turning the space inside the glass into a raging storm, smothering Cain and the others.

'Are you all right?' Isabel was shaking his arm. 'Are you hurt?'

Ash lay in a ball, arms wrapped round his head. His eyes were stinging from the dirt blasted there by the cloud that had barrelled into the lobby. Tears welled and spilt over, running down his cheeks. His mouth was full of grit.

'Say something.'

'I'm . . . OK.' He blinked and sat up. 'I think.' He rubbed his eyes and squinted at Isabel. She was covered in so much dust that her hair was now a greyish colour. Her face was streaked where tears had run through the grime. She looked as if she had just survived a hurricane – which was exactly how Ash felt.

All around them, the air was hazy. Dirt floated in a heavy fog, specks of it sparkling in the sunshine.

'Damn it.' Cain's voice in the lobby, boots crunching. 'How the hell do we get off this island now?'

Ash and Isabel dropped flat and slipped as far as they could under the counter.

'Don't you have someone you can call?' It was the older man who had spoken. The one in the dishevelled suit.

'Disable all communications.' Ash could tell Cain was trying to control her temper. 'Contain all personnel, and seal this place. By the time anyone comes to investigate, we'll have *Kronos* and be long gone. That's what we agreed, Pierce. All you wanted was what you've got in that bag, and that thing in the crate.'

Pierce. The name brought another flash of memory.

'*Pierce sent you.*' That's what Mum had said when Cain and the slender man came to the house. It was all coming back to Ash now.

The man in the dishevelled suit was Pierce.

'There's a boat,' Pierce said. 'On the other side of the island.'

'I knew there was a reason we brought you along.' Cain's voice was thick with sarcasm.

'Look, I'm in *charge* of—'

'There'll be a radio on the boat.' Cain cut him off. 'I can get a chopper here in well under an hour.'

'That means crossing the island on foot,' Pierce said. 'And this isn't just any island; there's a reason it's a black site. Devil's Island.' He grunted. 'There are things out there you can't even imagine.'

'There's no other choice. We'll lock this place down, get what we need from the residence, and bug out.'

'But Thorn is still in there. We can't just leave him. If he thinks we left him behind and then gets out, he'll gut us both.' Pierce sounded scared. 'My God, didn't you see what he did to those guards? And that man in the corridor? Thorn almost split him in half . . .'

Thorn. The name wrapped itself around Ash's heart and squeezed.

Ah. So now you remember how it started, said the voice. *Thorn came to the house with Cain. Pierce sent them for you. Thorn is the one who put the needle in your neck. The one without any expression, and a smooth, deep voice.*

Ash had seen into Thorn's expressionless eyes, and now shivered at the thought of what he might have done to the guard.

'Thorn knows the stakes,' Cain said. 'He can look after himself. We need to move.'

Boots crunched dirt against the tiled floor, then there was a tremendous clattering and Ash looked up at the ceiling to see thick steel shutters rolling out across the top of the dome.

Clatter-clunk, clatter-clunk.

By the time Ash gathered the courage to peer over the top of the wooden counter, the shutters were almost halfway down. Outside, the clearing was a foggy blur of smoke and dust, with six figures disappearing into it.

The shutters continued to lower until they finally reached

the ground, shutting out all the light, and coming to a terrible, shuddering stop. The steel encased the building like it was a giant metal tomb. Only a few glimmers of sunlight leaked through the links in the metal slats, dust hanging in the miniature rays.

After that, there was no sound in the lobby except for the beating of their hearts.

Behind the counter, Ash stared up at the shutters. 'Where's the lab? Mum and the others must still be there.'

Isabel nodded. 'This way.' She stood and turned without looking at Ash. She didn't want him to see her face, but Ash could tell she was trying to make herself calm, just like he was.

There was enough light for them to make out the bottom of the stairwell, but the floor was just a grey sea, so they couldn't tell what they were going to stand on next. The cloud of debris had scattered a shower of broken twigs and stones all over the floor. To Ash it felt like a carpet of crushed glass and rusty nails on the naked soles of his feet, so while Isabel moved ahead he was left to pick his way through.

'Slow down,' he called. 'This is killing my feet.'

Isabel stopped at the bottom of the stairs and waited for him to catch up. 'What happened to your clothes and shoes?'

'I wish I knew. That woman – Cain – she came to our house with a *really* scary guy called Thorn. Something to do with that older man, Pierce, and they were talking about "*Kronos*", whatever that is. Thorn hit me, smacked me down and stuck a needle in me and that's the last thing I remember. Drugged me, I think. Mum too.'

Isabel shook her head. 'I saw them take you off the helicopter. I thought you were sleeping.'

Ash swept the debris off the bottom step and sat down. He lifted his feet one after the other and dusted away the grit and splinters that were stuck to the soles. 'Was that really two days ago? I mean, how is that possible? How can I have slept for two days without waking up?' He turned to the stairwell, where the light was weaker and the landing was in darkness. 'I need to find my mum. We have to keep moving.'

Before they could take another step, though, a voice floated down. 'Pierce? Cain? What's going on?'

Ash would have recognized that soft, deep voice anywhere. It was the last thing he had heard before waking in the white room.

Thorn.

He imagined Thorn at the top of the stairs, staring down into the patchy light, his eyes like the dead, his face without expression. (*He'll gut us both.*) Ash remembered the fear in Pierce's voice.

'Hide.' He hardly even spoke the word. It came out more like a gentle breath.

'What?' Isabel lowered her voice to match his.

'You didn't hear that?'

'Hear what?'

'Thorn's coming. We have to hide.'

They crept back to the reception and slipped under the

counter again. Isabel was only a little taller than Ash so there was enough room for them to squash into the places that were flooded with shadow. Ash could hear gentle footsteps descending the stairs.

When Thorn reached the bottom, he stopped.

Ash imagined the man sniffing the air like an animal, listening for any sound. If this place had done something to his own senses, then perhaps it had done the same for Thorn's.

When Thorn moved again, Ash could hear only the slightest rustle. Despite the debris on the floor, he crossed the lobby in near silence, moving like a ghost.

Ash closed his eyes and listened to the whisper of footsteps heading towards the far wall and then around the curve of the lobby before they came to a stop. Again, there was a long moment of silence, then Thorn came in their direction.

All they could do was lie there and wait as Thorn came closer and closer until eventually he stepped behind the counter, bringing with him the smell of new leather and peppermint.

In a sudden moment of strange understanding, Ash realized he could hear the man's strong and steady heartbeat. His hearing focused in on it as if it were the only sound, and it gave Ash such a surprise that his eyes opened and he found himself looking at the toes of Thorn's boots, just a few centimetres from his nose.

Ash held his breath as the man ran his hands along the counter, then underneath until he touched a switch, no more than a metre above Ash's head.

He flicked it.

On. Off. On. Off.

Thorn sighed. 'Damn it; lockdown. Cain used the remote to close the shutters. But there must be another way out. There's *always* a way out.'

Once Thorn had found the shutter switch and confirmed it didn't work, he left, moving as quietly as he had arrived.

Ash and Isabel waited for what felt like at least another half an hour, until their legs had gone to sleep and their backs were stiff, before they moved. Thorn's smell lingered in Ash's nostrils, but Ash was sure about one thing; Thorn hadn't known they were there, and that meant his senses weren't working the way Ash's were. Whatever was happening to him, it wasn't happening to anyone else.

'We have to get to this lab you mentioned,' he said to Isabel. 'Someone there will know what to do.' But his mind was already starting to work against him. Dark thoughts reminded him what Pierce and Cain had been talking about before they left – their plan was to disable all communications and all personnel.

They're dead, the voice whispered in his head. *Everybody's dead.*

They emerged from behind the counter and made their way through the gloom towards the stairwell. As they climbed to the first landing, the faint light from the lobby faded to nothing, and when they turned to the next flight of stairs they saw only a never-ending blackness.

'There's no power anywhere?' Ash whispered. 'No . . . like, emergency lights or something?'

Isabel's dry throat clicked. '*No sé.* I don't know.'

'Maybe they switched it all off.' Ash felt the dread of knowing they had to go into the dark. 'Don't suppose you've got a torch or something?'

'Not here. At my house, yes, but—'

'Do you know the way to the lab, then? Can you get to it in the dark?'

'I don't know. Yes. Maybe. Papa showed me the way . . . once.'

'*Maybe?*'

'I mean, I think I can.'

'I suppose that'll have to do.' Ash climbed the first step, then stopped. 'We better hold onto each other.'

'What if he's there?' Isabel asked. 'That man.'

'He can't see in the dark.'

But that voice floated down from the tower in Ash's head, saying, *Maybe Thorn can see in the dark just fine.*

Maybe he's watching you right now.

Isabel stepped up beside him and took his hand. Her skin was warm, her palm sweaty. She squeezed Ash's fingers and Ash squeezed back.

'My name's Ash,' he said.

'OK, Ash,' she replied. 'Let's go.'

There were no sounds other than their own shuffling footsteps and heavy breathing. No feeling for Ash but the constant fear that he would step on something in his bare feet or walk into something left in the corridor.

They moved slowly and Ash put his right hand out in front of him, waving it up and down in an arc, like the fire safety guy had shown them at school. Isabel's fingers rasped along the wall to the left, sounding like something shuffling beside them – something maybe grinning with a mouth full of needle-like teeth as it waited for just the right moment to get them.

'You live here?' Ash tried to think about something else. 'And it's an island?'

'Yes.'

'Big or small?'

'I guess . . . small. But it takes two days to get from one end to the other. There are no roads.'

Ash imagined it as a green island in the middle of a crystal-blue sea, covered in thick jungle, with this building smack in the centre. 'And what's this place?'

'The BioSphere. It's for special research. Papa is a scientist.'

'Doing what? Did he ever mention something called "*Kronos*"?'

'Papa never tells me what work he is doing. It's . . . *secreto.*'

'Secret? You mean this place is some kind of secret research— Shh!' Ash stopped moving and his grip tightened.

'You hear something?' Isabel whispered.

'I thought . . .' Ash listened again, turning his head and breathing deeply. In that moment, he felt absurd; like an animal sniffing the air and listening for danger. 'No. Come on.'

'We came here six months ago,' Isabel told him. 'From San Jose. It was a good job for Papa. Good pay.'

'What about your mum?' Ash couldn't understand why he hadn't thought of it before. 'You said you have a house. Isn't your Mum there? She'll have heard the helicopter, and—'

A gentle click came from somewhere ahead.

Terror washed over Ash like an icy breeze. He pressed tight against the wall, pulling Isabel back so she was right beside him. 'Quiet.'

Another click was followed by the sound of soft footsteps. A tingling flooded through Ash's body, heightening his senses even further, making everything numb and alive all at once. Lights sparkled and danced in front of him as if tiny fireworks were flashing in his eyes. The smell of peppermint and new leather flooded his nostrils.

Thorn.

Ash held his breath as the slightest breeze wafted against his face; something was just centimetres away from them on the other side of the corridor. It couldn't see them, but perhaps it knew they were there, and all it had to do was reach out and it would have them. It would drag them away and do unspeakable things . . .

But then it moved. A creak of shoe leather, a waft of air, another gentle footstep followed by another until it receded into the darkness the way it had come.

Ash and Isabel waited in silence, neither of them daring to move until Ash leant over and made himself speak. 'We need to get moving.'

'Is he gone?'

'For now.'

They had no choice other than to keep going, so they set off again, skin prickling in anticipation of what might be creeping up behind them. Ash could hear his blood in his ears as if the world couldn't be completely silent in the way it could be completely dark. There was the gentle *pad-shtick* of his bare feet, and the *tap-tap* of Isabel's boots. The *swish* of cotton pyjamas as Ash waved his hand in front of him, up and down up and down. And there was the *shhhhh* of Isabel's fingers on the wall. Those noises filled his head like they were trying to drive him mad, and he reached up to touch the tag round his neck, to find the strength to bring everything under control.

'We are close now.' Isabel led Ash round the corner into a part of the building he had never seen.

They crept to the end of the corridor and eased the door

open on silent hinges. A powerful smell hit Ash like a blunt instrument, making him reel back and pull against Isabel.

'What is it?' she said. 'What's wrong?'

'Something . . .' he panted, trying to rid himself of that terrible smell. 'Something bad.'

'What?' Her voice was tight and high-pitched. 'What is it?'

It's death. It's DEATH!

'I don't know.' His chest hitched and everything felt constricted, as if he were underwater.

'Is it him?' Isabel's fingers squeezed in Ash's grip. 'Is it Thorn?'

'No . . .' Ash was beginning to lose control and had to stop himself. He couldn't afford to panic. They were alone and had to cope.

'What, then? What is it?'

'I don't know. Some kind of smell. It's like . . .'

(*Like the smell of a butcher's shop.*)

Ash put out his foot, stretching into the darkness until his toe came into contact with something blocking the corridor. Realizing straight away what it was, he lurched in horror, slipping on a warm and wet liquid. He fell flat on his backside, his hand ripping away from Isabel's, and panic threatened to crush the air out of him.

Isabel reached out, feeling across his chest with trembling fingers. She found his arm and followed it down to take his hand. 'What is it?' Her whisper was desperate and breathless. '*What's there?*'

Ash opened his mouth to speak, but nothing came out.

His lungs were tight, his throat narrow.

'Breathe,' she said. 'Breathe. It's OK. We are together, remember?'

Ash nodded and felt his breath return. 'A body,' he managed. 'I think it's a body.'

It's your mum, said the voice.

'**I**s it Papa?' Isabel asked.

'I don't know.' Ash was afraid and repulsed all at once. His first thought was to get away, but he stopped and tried to be calm. They had to know who it was.

He considered all the strange things that were happening to him, wondering if he could use it to his advantage. All those different smells, heightened and overwhelming . . . Maybe he could use that.

He took a shallow breath, focusing not on the blood but on the other things that mixed with it. Isabel's coconut, the faint remnant of peppermint, cleaning fluid, the hint of gun smoke. Perhaps he would be able to pick out something that would tell him if this was Mum.

Aftershave.

'I think it's a man,' he said before he could stop himself.

'Papa?' Isabel whispered.

Fighting his revulsion, Ash reached out to touch the body. He felt round the shoulder, then the neck, until he touched the face.

'Does your papa wear glasses?' he asked.

'No.'

Ash snatched his hand away and sat back. 'It's not him.'

'You're sure?'

'This man wears glasses.' He paused. 'Wore glasses.'

'*Gracias a Dios.*' Isabel grasped her new friend's arm. 'Thank you. Thank you for—' She stopped as if some great realization had just dawned on her. 'It must be Paco.'

'You know him?'

'Yes. He worked with Papa.'

'I . . .' Ash didn't know what to say.

Isabel cleared her throat and her words wavered when she spoke. 'The scientists, they have a card. A key to open the door into the lab.'

'A keycard? Why didn't you tell me before?'

'There's nowhere else to go. I thought maybe—'

'Doesn't matter.' Ash stopped her. 'I'll check.' He couldn't quite believe that he'd said it or that he was actually going to do it, but he reached out again until his fingers came into contact with the dead body. 'Where will the keycard be?' He kept his voice down, terrified of attracting the attention of whoever or whatever had passed them in the corridor not long ago.

'On the . . . how you say? *Cinturón*. On the trousers there is a thing for holding them up.'

'On the belt?'

'Yes. Belt.'

'OK.' Ash shuffled closer, feeling something wet soaking through the knee of his pyjamas.

IT'SBLOODIT'SBLOODIT'SBLOOD! the voice screamed in his head, and the smell of blood threatened to wash over him once more. He remembered Pierce's words and knew that this was what he had meant. Thorn had killed this man.

Thorn almost split him in half.

Fighting back the gagging in his throat, Ash slipped his hand along what he thought was the leg until he came to the thigh, then he moved his hand across the waist until he found the plastic holder clipped to the belt. He whipped it off, holding it tight in his fist.

'Right, let's get out of here.'

They joined hands once more and left the body behind them. They shuffled further into the abyss, deeper and deeper, until they came to the stairs, then they crept down several flights until, somewhere below, Ash saw a single red eye.

'What is that?' He tried not to imagine what kind of horrifying monster might be waiting for them in the darkness.

'There's still power to the locks,' Isabel said.

It took only a moment for Ash to realize what she meant – that the red light was not an eye, but the light on some kind of security lock. The card he had taken from the body would open it. He hoped.

'Papa said it's almost impossible to turn it off. For emergencies. It has its own battery.'

Gripping each other's hand, Ash and Isabel continued along the corridor, the red eye coming closer and closer, until they arrived at a dead end.

The double doors spanned the width of the corridor, but had no glass section like the others, so there was no way of looking through to see what was on the other side. 'Try the card,' Isabel said, and Ash took it from the plastic holder.

The red light on the lock glowed brighter when he looked down to find the slot, and he had no trouble inserting the card.

Beep!

The light flicked green and the lock clunked somewhere behind the door.

'That's it!' Isabel pushed forward and the door swung open, letting out a dull, blue glow.

Ash had never been so pleased to see even the smallest amount of light, but as they stepped into the lab, it dawned on him that they had heard a *lot* of shooting. Much more than was needed to kill the one man now lying in the corridor.

An awful feeling came over him.

Maybe everyone in the lab was dead; perhaps, other than Thorn, he and Isabel were the only ones left alive.

The lab was a billion miles away from the kind of thing they had at school. A clinical, icy-blue glow made everything feel hostile and alien, and the air smelt of polished metal and chemicals. Underneath that was the faint hint of another smell; like unburnt gas from a cooker.

As they ventured further into the lab, Ash saw a huge, circular corridor that made him think he was inside a giant stainless-steel doughnut, with the centre section divided into four wedge-shaped glass labs. Each lab was at least the size of a school hall, and was filled with equipment that wouldn't have looked out of place in a science fiction film. There were computers with dimly glowing keyboards, glass chambers with pipes connected to the metal ceilings, and row upon row of shiny containers that looked like large-calibre ammunition shells.

The nearest lab had robotic arms sprouting from the floor, pincers hanging over a dental chair that was surrounded by even more medical apparatus. Along one wall was a row of twelve metal-framed, glass-fronted cubicles, each one with a digital screen.

Large, black-haired monkeys occupied four of the cubicles. They had been pacing their prisons, but the moment Ash and Isabel came in, the monkeys stopped and came right up to the glass to watch. Standing up, the creatures would have been almost as tall as Ash, but they remained hunched, with powerful shoulders drawn forwards. Their sleek hair shone, and each had a grey stripe across its back, shimmering in the eerie blue light. They ignored Isabel, fixing their eyes on Ash.

Close to the door of the lab where the monkeys were imprisoned, two security guards lay face down on the floor, with blood pooled around them. Ash knew they were more of Thorn's victims.

'Papa must be in one of the other labs.' Isabel's voice was small and quiet. She let go of Ash's hand and moved ahead, her pace quickening as she hurried round the circular corridor, boots clomping on the metallic floor.

Ash went after her, catching up as they rounded the bend and the third lab came into view. What they saw made them stop in their tracks.

Inside, Mum was leaning against a large waist-high glass box with four holes in the front. Her arms were crossed and her head was hanging as if she were deep in thought.

On the opposite side of the room, an olive-skinned man was standing beside a tall clear-fronted refrigerator filled with small bottles of amber liquid. He wore a pass clipped to his belt, his name printed in small type on it: *Dr Ernesto Vasquez*. Isabel's papa. Close to him, two women were sitting cross-legged on the floor.

They were all wearing yellow protective hazmat suits without the helmets.

Ash came to a halt as if he had run into an invisible barrier. The relief of seeing his mum alive was incredible.

'Papa!' Isabel shouted, but there was no reaction from anyone inside the lab, so she knocked hard on the glass. 'Maria? Begonia?'

Ash's mum jerked her head up and caught sight of her son. She looked tired, with hunched shoulders and blood-shot eyes, and her face was glistening as if it were too hot in the lab. When she saw Ash, though, she pushed away from the in-vitro cabinet and hurried forward. The two women got to their feet, and Isabel's dad rushed towards the thick glass wall.

As soon as Ash locked eyes with his mum, he began to speak, letting everything pour out. 'What's happening? There was shooting and there's dead people, and we came through the corridor in the dark and something weird is happening to me, I can hear and smell things that . . .' He was babbling but couldn't stop himself. It was such a relief to find his mum alive.

Beside him, Isabel was talking to her dad in Spanish,

telling him more or less the same thing, but both Ash's mum and Isabel's dad were shaking their heads and pointing to their ears.

Then Ash's mum made a fist and banged hard on the glass. She held up a hand, telling him to stay put, and reached to the desk behind her. Picking up a tablet computer, she typed something before showing it to her son.

Soundproof. Room sealed.

Ash grabbed Isabel's shoulder to stop her from talking. 'It's soundproof,' he told her. 'They can't hear us.'

Isabel stopped and glared at him like she was going to hit him – like it was his fault or something – so Ash pointed at his mum. 'Look.'

Isabel turned to see the message and stood there, staring at it, not knowing what to do. 'Why is it sealed? What is wrong?'

'I don't know.' Some of the relief at having found Mum began to slide away.

Find tablet in other lab.

Ash nodded and Isabel hurried with him to the lab where the monkeys were locked in their cells. The animals stared at him with their piercing green eyes, but Ash ignored them as he searched the room. He finally spotted a tablet computer lying on a pristine white surface next to a glass oven.

'Here,' he said to Isabel as he grabbed it and rushed back.

As soon as he was ready, Mum typed: **I couldn't wake you. Had to give IV drip. Are you hurt?**

Ash read the words, then looked down a̶

dressed only in pyjamas and covered in bloc̶

bered pulling the needle from his hand and̶

him he had been there for two days. He wantec̶

many things, but first he had to let his mum know he ̶

OK.

Not my blood.

'Why is the room sealed?' Isabel leant over his shoulder,
pointing at the screen. 'Ask why the—'

'I am.' His fingers fumbled, missing some of the letters:
Why s room sealed? Com out.

Mum put a hand to her mouth, then composed herself:
Get help.

From where? Who? How?

Have you seen anyone else?

'Why doesn't she answer the question?' Isabel grabbed
the top of the tablet computer and pulled it closer.

'Please.' Ash tugged it back and typed: **Pierce. Cain.
Thorn.** He remembered the names as if they were burnt
into his brain. **No one else I recognized. Big man. Hulk.
3 others.**

Where are P, C & T now?

I don't know.

Think. This is very important. Are they near?

Ash looked at Isabel and bit his lip. He thought about the
horrible journey from the lobby to the lab. **Thorn still here.
Others gone.**

In the helicopter?

Crashed, he typed in reply. **2 men in helicopter. Don't**

r dead. 1 person dead in corridor. 2
by other lab. No power. No phones. Shut-
how can we get help? Ash was trying to stay
give Mum as much information as he could. Mum
stared at his words until he took the tablet away and
stabbed again at the virtual keyboard on the screen: **Please
cpome out now!**

Mum pursed her lips and continued to stare. She took a
deep breath and finally looked down at her own tablet:
Where did Cain and Pierce go?

I don't know.

'*¡Madre de Dios!*' Isabel threw her hands in the air. '*¿Por
qué no vienen a cabo?* Why won't they come out? Give it
to me. Let me ask Papa.' She reached towards the tablet
computer.

'Wait.' Ash turned his body to stop her from taking it, then
typed: **What's going on? Why is room sealed? Why
don't you come out?**

When he held it up, Mum stood there, with her tablet in
one hand, but she didn't type anything. She just stared at him
again, eyes glistening, so Ash went closer to the glass and
thrust the tablet towards it, clenching his jaw and furrowing
his brow. He wanted her to see that he was scared.

When Mum didn't answer straight away, Ash added
something else and held it out for her to see. **Who are
Cain and Pierce and Thorn? What is happening to me?
What is Kronos?**

Mum deflated. Her shoulders dropped and she hung her
head like she was beaten. When she looked up again, her

face was bathed in the lab's pale blue light, giving her a ghoulish appearance. She made herself smile, but her eyes flickered and she glanced over her son's shoulder, making Ash and Isabel turn to look behind them.

'Oh no.' Isabel wilted.

'What?' Ash asked. 'What is it?'

'There.' Isabel tipped her head towards a large console against the far wall. It displayed a complicated array of dials and buttons and blinking lights, but that wasn't what Mum was looking at. She was looking at the four yellow helmets lying beside it.

A connection began to form in Ash's mind, bringing together the hazmat suits without helmets, the sealed lab door and the look on Mum's face

When they turned back to Mum, she was holding up another message for them.

Kronos is a virus. Very dangerous and contagious. Deadly. Pierce and others have stolen it.

Beside him, Isabel took a sudden sharp breath. Her heart quickened in her chest – *ba-dum, ba-dum, ba-dum* – and Ash heard it as clearly as if someone were beating a drum right next to him. It was the strangest thing; being able to hear her heart like that. It increased his confusion and he could only stare as Mum typed a new message.

Don't know why they want it. But if it is released, millions will die. We tried to stop him.

Millions will die? Ash read the words over and over.

With trembling fingers, he typed again. **Is it in there with you?**

Mum looked away, tears coming to her eyes. She moved the tablet as if she were going to type something, but stopped, fingers hovering over the screen. She bowed her head and her shoulders hitched, so Isabel's dad gently took the tablet from her.

Pierce locked us in here. Released the virus into this room, scrambled lock code. He has only keycard to open it.

Isabel took a step back, a look of horror spreading across her face. '*Un remedio. Debe haber un remedio.*'

The world swam around Ash like a liquid dream. He was aware of Isabel beside him; could feel her reaction, hear her heart pounding. He could actually *smell* fear oozing from her pores with the scent of burnt plastic. All thoughts of what was happening to him were gone as he typed once more.

Cure?

Dr Vasquez frowned. **Antiviral is called Zeus. Pierce brought Dr McCarthy here to make it. Now he has it. Took everything. Has virus, antiviral, vaccine, all the research, leaving island.**

Ash glanced at his mum, then typed: **Make more antiviral.**

Dr Vasquez shook his head. **We don't have everything we need. No way to get it in here. Lab is locked.**

Isabel sobbed. Her knees buckled and she sank to the floor. Ash knew exactly how she felt, but didn't know what to say to her. He set the tablet to one side and put an arm around her shoulder. Mum had comforted him many times since Dad had died, sitting exactly like this, not saying anything, because sometimes there isn't anything you *can* say. It might help if there is someone to share it with you, someone to strengthen you, but sometimes you have to accept things for what they are; learn to live with them.

But Ash decided this wasn't going to be one of those times. There was nothing he could do about what had happened to Dad – he couldn't bring him back – but there had to be something he could do to help Mum. There *had* to be.

Dad wouldn't have given up, so neither would he.

'We can get it back,' he said to Isabel. 'The cure. The keycard.'

'How?'

'There has to be *some*thing.' He wasn't going to lose his mum without a fight, and he began to feel the same things he had felt when he saw Cain attacking her that day after the funeral – all that anger, determination and fear mixing up into a powerful potion that put a raging fire in him. 'We have to do something,' he said. 'We can't give up. We have to be tough. We have to be clever.' He wanted Isabel to feel the same fire inside her. 'You got us to the lab in the dark. You're brave, I know you are, so come on, Isabel, think. What can we do?'

'I don't know . . . They said they're going to cross the island and be gone. Maybe we could go after them, if—'

'That's it!' Ash jumped to his feet as a memory of the helicopter popped into his mind. 'You're a genius. They *can't* just leave the island. They have to *cross* it. We can go after them. And they're carrying that crate – they'll be slow!

Isabel shook her head and stopped him. 'I am sorry, Ash. You are forgetting lockdown. The shutters. We can't get out of here.'

Ash stopped with his mouth open and cold dread rose through him. 'But there *has* to be another way out,' he said. 'It doesn't make sense to be able to shut everything down like that.'

'It's for safety. In case—'

'A way to open the shutters, then.'

Isabel held out her hands. 'I . . . I don't know.'

'Another door? Emergency exit? *Some*thing?'

'No, I . . .'

Ash fought back tears of frustration as he turned away and jabbed at the keyboard on the tablet computer. **Pierce and Cain crossing island to boat. We could try to stop them but everything locked down. Shutters everywhere. No power but here. How do we get out?**

Mum stared at the words, then raised her eyes to look at her son. It was the clearest expression of desolation Ash had ever seen. She would die in the lab, while Ash and Isabel watched. Eventually food would run out, water would run out, and then they too would die.

But Isabel's dad typed something and held it up for Isabel to read.

Use HEX13

'Is that a way out?' Ash felt a glimmer of fresh hope. 'Like a door or something?'

'Yes.' Isabel narrowed her eyes as she thought about it. 'A

way out.'

'Then what are we waiting for? Let's go.'

Mum and Dr Vasquez shared a glance before Mum took the tablet. **No**, she typed. **Too dangerous.**

We have to do *something*! Ash replied.

Mum shook her head.

What else can we do? Stay here?

Mum read the words and looked away. He was right. He couldn't stay in the lab and watch her die.

I am Ash McCarthy, he wrote. **I am strong. I can do this.**

Ash put the tablet up against the glass until his mum looked to see what he had written. When she did, tears welled in her eyes. She knew the words and she knew what they meant to him.

I won't lose you too, Ash wrote.

Mum lowered her head with a heavy sigh. When she looked up again, she met her son's gaze for a second, then turned and spoke to Isabel's dad.

'What are they saying?' Isabel was watching them intently, trying to read their lips, but she could only make out the odd word. 'Can you tell?'

'No. Are they arguing?' Ash thought there were some moments when they might be, and others when they seemed to agree. The two women joined the conversation, coming together so the four of them were standing in a huddle in the centre of the lab.

'They are making a decision,' Isabel said.

'Yeah. But about what?'

Eventually they nodded to one another, shook hands, and then Mum came forward and typed another message while the others watched.

Boat is in bay on other side of island. Isabel knows it. You must get to it before Pierce. Damage it. Destroy it. Stop them getting on boat. They MUST NOT leave island.

Ash nodded, excited by their sudden burst of optimism. **We will bring cure and keycard.**

When Mum read his message, Ash was confused to see the look of sadness still on her face as she typed something else and held it up.

Most important is that they don't leave island. It is a priority. Kronos must be destroyed.

Ash read the three sentences over and over, feeling certain that he had missed something. From the look on Mum's face, he knew something wasn't right about this. Why was she so insistent about— And then it hit him. She was telling him to stop Pierce from taking *Kronos* off the island, not telling him to save her. If *Kronos* left the island, millions of people could die – that's what she wanted him to stop.

Mum didn't expect him to bring back the cure and the keycard. She wasn't expecting to be saved.

I can do this, he typed. **I will bring it back. I promise.**

Mum sobbed and turned her back on him. She walked to the far end of the lab and stood for a moment. Isabel's dad put a hand on her arm and they spoke quietly. When they were finished, Mum stood up straighter and returned to the glass. She typed a message and held it up for Ash to see.

There is no time. We have only a little more than 24 hours until Shut-Down. That is when our organs will begin to fail and the antiviral will not work for us. It is already too late. No more questions. You have to go. You *MUST* stop Pierce leaving the island. You MUST destroy the boat. You *MUST* destroy Kronos.

Ash read the message over and over until he could have spoken it word for word. When he could look at it no longer, he took a deep breath and turned to Isabel. 'We can do this, right?'

Isabel swallowed hard and fixed her most determined expression. 'Yes,' she said. 'We can. We *must*.'

'OK, then, we should go now. We don't have much time.'

Ash typed one more message and placed the tablet computer on the metal floor by his feet, turning it so the scientists could read what he had written. He nodded to his mum and looked at her for the last time before heading out of the lab.

When Ash and Isabel reached the door, the tablet screen had already dimmed, preparing to close down and conserve its battery, but the message was still visible:

I will come back. I will save you. I promise.

23 hrs and 45 mins until Shut-Down

'Twenty-four hours.' Isabel set the countdown timer on her digital watch. 'And we were in there for . . . fifteen minutes?'

Ash nodded, and when Isabel thumbed the button, the minutes began to tick away. Time was already running out. 'You sure you know where we're going?' he asked. 'HEX13?'

They sneaked back upstairs, bathed in the white glow of a handheld fluorescent light taken from one of the labs. Ash worried it would make them easy to spot, that Thorn would see them coming, but Isabel said she couldn't make it to the other end of the building without it. In a way, it was a relief not to be in total darkness, but Ash still had a prickle down the back of his head when he thought about Thorn being just beyond the light, so he reached out with all his senses, trying to detect him.

'Twenty-four hours is not long,' Isabel said.

'Just *over* twenty-four hours.' Ash tried not to think about Mum locked in that room with *Kronos* swimming in her blood.

'Maybe it's not enough.'

'It *is* enough,' Ash said. 'It's a whole day.'

'And even if we get out—'

'*When* we get out,' Ash corrected her. 'And don't think about it. Just get us out of here and we'll find Cain and Pierce, and get the cure. We'll be all right. We have to be.'

'Yes. We have to—' Isabel gasped and came to a stop.

On the floor just in front of them was a red footprint facing in their direction. It was faint, like a print in wet sand just on the edge of the shore, but it was clear enough to see the heel, the curve of the arch, the ball and the toes. Behind it was another, and then another, each one a little more visible than the last.

Ash's footprints. Not his blood, though.

And there were other prints too, from shoes or boots too large to be Isabel's.

'Thorn,' Isabel said.

'Ignore it.' Ash tried to sound brave. 'We already know he's here somewhere.'

Isabel nodded. 'That body – Paco – is up here, isn't he?'

Already, Ash could see a dark shape in the gloom on the floor ahead, and he could smell blood in the air. There was a hint of peppermint and leather too – Thorn's smell. It was swirling in a shimmer of chemicals, tropical fruit and fear. 'Look away,' he said. 'We'll go past.'

Paco was lying slumped against the wall. There was blood down the front of his white coat, a heavy patch of it around his stomach (*he'll gut us both*) and a puddle on the floor beside him. Ash could see where he had knelt when he was searching for the keycard, and the place where he had stepped in the man's blood before walking away.

'Look at the wall,' he told Isabel, and they left the horror behind, continuing past the lobby stairwell and along several other corridors leading into the darkness.

'Where's everyone else?' Ash whispered.

'There is no one else.'

'There's no one else on this island? No one at *all*?'

'Just Papa and me. Maria and Begonia and . . . and Paco. And a security team. Sometimes more guards come if there is a big project.'

'And you live here?' Ash asked. 'But how old are you? What about school?'

'I'm fourteen. Papa teaches me. Science. Maths and English.'

'And your mum?'

'I have no mama.' Isabel said it like she didn't want to talk about it, so Ash stopped asking questions and just followed for a while, the white light from the fluorescent bulb illuminating the way.

Isabel led them down the third corridor on the right, all the way to the door at the end, passing the mangled bodies of two more security guards, and when Ash put the card into the slot beside the door, something clunked inside. 'Still power to the locks,' he said. 'I wonder how long it lasts.'

Isabel shook her head and pushed on the door, stepping into a huge concrete room that smelt of dust and cardboard and a jumble of other things Ash didn't recognize. It was filled with shelving that reached from floor to ceiling, and had the open, empty feeling of a cave. The glow from the fluorescent tube reached only a couple of metres around them, and there was no sight of the far wall.

'I sometimes come in here with Dad to get supplies,' Isabel said. 'Always makes me feel . . . Brrr.' She shivered.

'You mean it gives you the creeps?' Ash looked around, squinting into the darkness beyond the light.

'The creeps. Yes.'

'Me too.'

They stole like thieves between two banks of shelves stacked high with orange plastic containers that looked like petrol cans, tins, spools of wire, jars of powders and pills. Even boxes containing cans of food. There were huge crates with images of medical equipment stuck on them, and rows and rows of the stainless-steel temperature-controlled containers they had seen in the labs.

Approaching an area stacked with tools, Isabel gave Ash the light, telling him to hold it close to the shelf so she could find what she was looking for – a red crowbar as long as her arm.

'What do we need that for?'

'You'll see.' Hefting the crowbar, Isabel took Ash to the back of the room where there was an endless line of metal cabinets. Each was taller than Ash, painted olive green and with a yellow number stencilled onto the door. Isabel counted along the row, '*Uno . . . dos . . . tres . . . quatro . .*' touching each cabinet as she went. When she came to number seventeen, she stopped and stood in front of it, crowbar hanging at her side.

'This one,' she said.

Ash watched in confusion. 'I thought we were looking for the way out?'

'We are.'

'And it's in there? What is it, some kind of secret entrance? It looks too small.'

'You'll see.' Isabel lifted the crowbar and slotted the narrow end into the crack in the cabinet, just above the lock. She put as much force behind it as she could, pushed and pushed, but nothing happened.

'You're never going to open it like that,' Ash said. 'Are you sure this is the way out?'

'This' – Isabel puffed as she leant on the crowbar – 'is the *only* way out. We need what's in here.' She held tight with both hands and jerked her weight against the bar, two, three times, but the locker door didn't budge.

'What is it? Some kind of key?'

'Just help me with this.' Isabel waggled the crowbar, trying to jam it deeper into the gap, and levered at the door once more. She grunted with effort, then stopped to catch her breath. 'Are you going to help me or not?'

'All right.' Ash put the light on the floor. He wasn't big for his age – not as strong as most of his friends – so he wasn't sure he'd do any better than Isabel, but he grabbed the crowbar, and—

From somewhere among the racks of supplies came a scuffing sound that made Ash snap his head up and look into the darkness.

'You heard that?' he whispered.

'I don't think so. You have good hearing.'

Ash nodded and held the crowbar back over his shoulder, ready to swing it hard like a cricket bat. 'It feels like someone is watching us,' he said. 'You feel that?'

'Maybe.'

He tightened his grip on the crowbar and listened, searching for the source of the sound. He strained his ears for the faint thrum of a heartbeat, or the soft sigh of a breath. He tested the air, detecting a trace of the horribly familiar scent of peppermint.

'Thorn?' he called. 'Is that you?'

Nothing.

'Come on,' Isabel said. 'Let's open this and get out of here.'

Ash waited a little longer, then nodded and turned back to the locker. It felt wrong to be facing away from whatever danger was out there, but Isabel was right. They had to get away fast. Ash had to think about saving Mum. If he concentrated on her, remembered how she had looked, how scared *she* was, then he could be strong. He could do this.

He turned and jammed the crowbar into the gap above the lock, looking at Isabel and saying, 'Together.'

One more hard shove was all it took. There was a crack as the lock snapped, and a bang as the door swung open and slammed back against the locker beside it. Isabel and Ash stumbled forwards, dropping the crowbar with a loud clatter that echoed through the room, jarring his sensitive hearing. At the same time, part of the lock shot away and pinged against the shelving. Ash put his hands on the bank of lockers to the left, stopping himself from smashing into them face first, and Isabel smacked into him from behind so that her head was right next to his, her chin on his shoulder.

Her heart was thumping so hard Ash could feel it against his back as well as hear it.

'You all right?' he asked.

'*Sí.*' Isabel nodded, her hair tickling his face, and then did the weirdest thing. She laughed.

It took Ash by surprise. There was nothing funny about what was happening. They were stuck in a research facility, in the dark, with a deadly virus and a lunatic killer on the loose. And he was still in his pyjamas. There was nothing funny about it *AT ALL*.

But Isabel's laugh was as infectious as *Kronos* and Ash couldn't stop himself from joining her. It was better than crying. Better than curling up in a ball and wishing they were safe. So they stayed there, leaning against the locker, laughing away the fear and horror of the past hour.

'I think we did it,' Ash said, finally coming to his senses. 'I think it's open.'

Still leaning against him, Isabel stifled her giggling. 'You're stronger than you look.' She became serious, as if remembering where they were and what they had to do.

Ash did the same and looked at the box nestled in the bottom of the locker.

It was metal, olive green, with writing stencilled on the top:

DANGER. HIGH EXPLOSIVES.

Ash stepped back. 'Seriously? That's our way out? Explosives?'

Isabel picked up the light and held it towards the locker, peering inside. 'You could read that?' she asked. 'Without the light?'

'Yeah.' Ash was confused. 'It's just there. I mean . . .' His eyes locked with Isabel's.

'You hear good *and* you see good,' she said.

Ash shrugged. 'I guess. Yeah.'

He glanced back at the locker, wondering what was happening to him. How had he been able to read the stencilling and Isabel hadn't? In the total darkness of the corridor he had been as blind as Isabel, but with just a little light, he could see better. He wished there had been time to ask Mum about it. Maybe it was something to do with *Kronos*. Or the BioSphere. Whatever it was, it was freaky, but at least it was becoming easier to control.

Isabel was staring at him as if she were trying to figure him out, so Ash changed the subject. 'You're serious about this? We're going to *blow* our way out?'

'Yes.'

'No way. I mean, it's kind of cool, but there has to be something else. An emergency door or . . . something.'

Isabel blinked and looked down at the box. 'In lockdown, everything is closed. *Everything.* This is the only way out.'

'We'll kill ourselves.'

Isabel placed the light on the ground, and reached in to unfasten the catch on the front of the box. When she popped it open, the scent of marzipan oozed out.

'Careful.' Ash took another step back.

'It's safe,' Isabel said. 'I've used it before.'

'You've used it *before*? Why? Why is it even here?'

'It's something new,' Isabel said. 'For research.'

'That doesn't make sense. I thought this place was for, like, medicines and stuff.'

Isabel glanced up at him. 'This *is* stuff.'

'No, this is weapons. They make weapons here?'

'Not guns. Other kinds of weapons, I think.'

Ash tried to digest what Isabel was telling him. 'Other things like what?'

'Like this, I guess.'

'And why have *you* used it?'

'Well.' She shrugged and leant back to let Ash see what was in the box. 'Papa tested it and I watched. Out in the jungle. It's very safe until it's ready to . . .'

'Explode?'

'Yes. Or flash or smoke. It can do many things. Soon it will be for the army to use, I think.'

'The army? My God.' Ash rubbed a hand over his head. 'This place is getting crazier by the minute.' He paused, trying to make sense of everything. 'Anyway, you said your dad didn't talk about his work.'

'Well . . . he is not supposed to. I'm not really allowed in the lab or to know what they are doing, but he told me about this. Said it was fun and let me watch him test it.'

Ash took a step closer and studied the contents of the metal container. At one end was a number of what looked like plastic pencil boxes, while the rest was stacked with bricks wrapped in brown paper. Each brick had HEX13 printed on the top.

'High Explosives Experiment Number Thirteen,' Isabel explained.

'What does that mean? That it took them thirteen tries to get it right?'

'Yes.'

'Sheesh.' Ash shook his head. 'You sure it's safe?'

'It won't go off without these.' Isabel took out one of the small plastic boxes, and opened it to show Ash what appeared to be a smartphone and a collection of metal matchsticks. 'They're . . . how you say . . . ?' She waggled her index finger like she was firing a gun.

'Triggers?' Ash tried to sound brave and like he knew what he was talking about, but he couldn't stop thinking that he was standing in front of a box full of *explosives*!

'Detonators.' Isabel tapped the metal sticks as she remembered the word she was looking for. 'And this is the handset.' She picked up the object that looked like a smartphone. 'We take them with us to the shutters and make a hole.'

'Just like that?'

Isabel shrugged. 'It only needs a little.'

'What about using it to get them out of that lab, then? To break the glass?'

'I think it would be too dangerous. Maybe kill them.'

A clear and horrible picture popped into Ash's head – of Mum and the others blown apart inside the lab. 'Yeah, you're probably right.'

'So.' Isabel grabbed a satchel from beside the metal box containing the HEX13, then opened it wide so they could place the bricks inside. 'Let's do it.'

But as Ash reached out to take the first one, he realized he had made a mistake. While he had been worrying about explosions and escape, he had failed to notice something important. His own heart drummed in his chest, steady and firm. Beside him, Isabel's beat harder and faster.

But they had been joined by a third heartbeat. A slow and strong rhythm accompanied by the strong scent of peppermint and new leather . . .

Ash whipped round, as a soft voice spoke from the darkness.

'I think you kids better let me take over now.'

23 hrs and 09 mins until Shut-Down

Ash's hand went down, feeling for the crowbar lying on the floor.

'That looks like dangerous stuff.' The voice again. Smooth and deep. 'You'll kill yourselves.' Something stepped closer to the edge of the semi-circle of white light. It was just a silhouette, but Ash recognized the slender shape.

'Thorn.' The word escaped his mouth before he realized he was going to say it.

'Give it to me and I'll get you out of here.'

Isabel backed up against the lockers, breathing hard.

'No . . .' Ash managed to say. He was both afraid and annoyed with himself for allowing Thorn to creep up on them. 'You . . . injected me. My mum too.'

Thorn took a small step closer, making hardly a sound. 'An unfortunate necessity. But you're all right, aren't you? I made sure of that.'

'You killed Paco,' Isabel stuttered. 'And the guards. Gave Papa the virus.'

'The virus?' Thorn took another step forward. 'No. Cain did that. And Pierce.'

'You're one of them,' Ash said as his fingers touched the cold metal of the crowbar.

'You're wrong about me, Ash.' Thorn's voice was quiet and soft. He was like a snake hypnotizing its prey. 'Let me *help* you.' He reached forward, his hand breaking into the light as if it were just floating there. 'We'll find a way out, together. *Trust* me.'

Ash tightened his grip around the crowbar and tensed his arm, ready to use it. Thorn took another step closer and Ash saw something metallic glint in the torchlight. The blade of a knife.

Thorn almost split him in half, Pierce had said.

Ash remembered the dead guards, the blood, and acted without further hesitation. He raised the crowbar as if it were no more than a large stick, and threw it at Thorn as hard as he could. After that, everything dropped into bizarre, frame-by-frame slow motion. Ash had time to watch the crowbar tumble, spinning lengthways as it crossed the distance to the edge of the semi-circle of light. He saw Thorn's shadow standing motionless, the crowbar heading towards him like a propeller, and when it was only a metre away Thorn began to react. He must have moved like lightning, even though it looked so much slower to Ash.

Thorn bent at the knees, then twisted and started to shift sideways, but he wasn't quick enough. The curved end of the tool struck his right shoulder, and Ash saw the wrinkle in the material of his jacket. The crowbar jerked when it made contact, flicking up so the straight end caught Thorn on the chin. Ash had time to see the ripple spread out across his cheek and his neck, then Thorn went down with a grunt, disappearing into the darkness.

A rush of air and the world hurried back into real time with a sharp clang as the crowbar hit the floor, and a clatter as Thorn's knife spun away to be lost beneath the shelving.

All Ash could do was crouch there, staring at the space where Thorn had been standing. He couldn't believe what he had done. What had felt like ten seconds must have happened in the blink of an eye.

'You got him,' Isabel said. 'You . . . you *hit* him.' Her words were tight and breathless.

Ash stared at the spot where Thorn had been standing. 'I killed him?'

'I don't think so. Just hit him.'

As if to confirm it, a long groan came from the shadows.

'We have to get away.' Isabel reached into the locker, taking the first block out of the metal box and shoving it into the satchel. 'He's waking up.' She grabbed another two, jamming them in, then threw in a box of detonators and took hold of Ash's arm. 'We must go.'

'Yes.' Ash shook himself, still trying to understand what

he had done; how he had moved so quickly and felt so strong.

'Come on.' Isabel threw the satchel over her shoulder. 'We have to get out of here. Leave him in the dark.'

Ash nodded and snatched up the light before they took off, hurrying between the shelves, racing along the length of the storage facility towards the way out. Somewhere behind them, Thorn groaned again and tried to get to his feet.

It wouldn't be long before he came after them – they didn't have much time . . .

Sprinting past the rack where the tools were stored, Ash glanced over at them, an idea forming. 'This might give us some time.'

He grabbed a second crowbar without breaking stride, and continued along the length of the cavernous store-room. Isabel's boots thundered on the concrete floor and their panting echoed around them. By the time they reached the exit, Ash was ahead, running so fast that he slammed into the doors, arms out to avoid hurting himself. He grabbed the handles, yanking them open, and the two of them rushed out into the corridor. Ash then turned to push the doors shut and slip the crowbar through the handles.

'That should slow him down.'

They ran and ran, blundering on with only the cocoon of light around them. Isabel stayed just ahead, picking out the right way to go, and Ash followed close behind, watching the satchel bouncing about on her back.

Boom! the voice kept saying in his head. That sneering

voice, floating down from the dark tower in his mind. *Boom! She's got a bomb on her back.*

When they came to the lobby stairwell, they raced down, taking the stairs two at a time, turning the corner then jumping the final few steps. Debris from the helicopter crash dug into the soles of Ash's feet as they hurried over to the building's entrance. Without power, the sliding doors remained firmly shut. Isabel shucked the pack from her back and crouched to remove one of the bricks of explosives. She was breathing heavily.

'You're not tired?' she asked.

'No.' Ash dismissed the comment. 'You sure you know what you're doing?'

'I saw Papa do this.' She tore off the brown paper to reveal a firm, white putty underneath.

'Careful.' Ash took a step back, expecting it to explode in Isabel's hands as she twisted off a piece the size of a matchbox. She squashed it flat and stuck it onto the glass doors like a giant blob of used chewing gum.

'Is that enough?' Ash asked.

'It's powerful.'

'Oh.' He winced and took a step back.

When she was done, Isabel reached into the satchel and took out one of the metal matchstick detonators. She pushed it into the putty and switched on the trigger device that looked like a smartphone.

It burst into life, displaying a large red button on the touchscreen with the word P A I R on it. Isabel tapped it once. Immediately, a tiny green light appeared at the end of the matchstick detonator. At the same time, three words materialized on the device's touchscreen.

HE
FLASH
SMOKE

'Do you know what they all mean?' Ash peered over her shoulder, then glanced back at the stairwell.

'Mm-hm.' Isabel nodded. 'This one is High Explosive.' She touched HE which flashed once before it was replaced with two other words.

TIMER
MARK

Isabel touched MARK, and a white dot began tracing across the screen in a 'Z' pattern. The word CONFIRM appeared above it.

'I think that's it,' Isabel said.

'You *think*? God, I hope you're right about this.'

'Me too.'

Ash took a deep breath and shook his head in disbelief. 'OK. What now?'

Isabel looked at Ash and blinked hard. There was sweat on her brow and determination in her eyes. 'We get back. Right back.'

'Behind the counter?' he asked.

'Further.'

'The stairs?'

Isabel got to her feet and picked up the satchel. 'Further.' Without waiting for Ash, she started walking back to the stair-well, taking strong, purposeful strides. 'Bring the flashlight.'

Ash was glad to see Isabel being tough. She had taken control of the HEX13, and looked stronger now than she had in the lab. It was as if she had realized there was no point in being scared and hoping someone would come to help them. No one was coming except Thorn. Seeing Isabel like that made him feel better, and he snatched up the light and jogged after his friend, picking through the debris and heading along the corridor at the top of the stairs.

They continued to the end, past room X, where it had all started for Ash, and crouched with their backs against the solid wall.

'This is it.' Isabel took a deep breath.

'Will it be loud?' he asked.

Isabel nodded, and Ash knew he had to prepare for the worst. With his senses as crazy as they were, there was a good chance this was going to hurt. A lot.

They stared at each other for a moment, then both looked down at the device in Isabel's hand.

'You've seen this before,' Ash said. 'You know what you're doing. I trust—'

Clang! From somewhere deep in the building came a metallic sound, followed by doors rattling.

'He's trying to get out!' Ash said.

Isabel moved her thumb so it was hovering over the touchscreen.

Another loud *CLANG*!

Ash imagined Thorn, face twisted in anger, swinging an axe at the door, breaking it from its hinges.

'The door's too strong,' Isabel said. 'Isn't it?'

'Yeah. Of course. I'm sure it is. Definitely.'

'But what if he uses the HEX13?'

'It's experimental isn't it?' Ash said. 'Even if he can find it in the dark, it'll take him time to work out how to use it. Come on, let's do this and get out of here.'

Isabel focused on the trigger device in her shaking hand. The white glow continued to move in a 'Z' shape across the screen with the word CONFIRM along the top. It repeated the pattern, waiting for Isabel to trace it, but she couldn't get her thumb to move.

'*Do it,*' Ash said.

It was their only hope. The only way they were ever going to get out. The only way to help his mum and Isabel's dad. The only way to stop Pierce from taking *Kronos* off the island.

Millions will die.

'I can't,' Isabel said. 'I can't move.' Her voice wavered in panic.

The banging continued, echoing through the corridors. It was growing louder and more terrifying with every passing moment. Thorn was like an angry caged beast, and with every second he was coming closer to escape.

Isabel was struggling to keep the device still, her whole hand jittering about. Ash put his own trembling hands around Isabel's, his thumb over the top of hers, and looked into her eyes.

They would do it together.

Unable to cover his ears, Ash prepared himself for the

painful noise and began to count. 'One.'

The banging continued. *Clang! Clang!* Over and over again.

'Two.'

'Three.' Ash pushed Isabel's thumb onto the touchscreen and together they traced the 'Z'.

The effect was instantaneous.

22 hrs and 42 mins until Shut-Down

The HEX13 exploded with a tremendous *BOOM!* The floor trembled as the sound and shock wave expanded from the lobby. Even where Ash and Isabel had taken cover, up two flights of stairs and all the way at the end of the corridor, something in the air changed. The oxygen was drawn away, making it impossible to breathe, and then it was sucked back in a blast of warm, scorched gases.

A sharp pain stabbed through Ash's head as it was filled with the sound of the explosion, but in an instant everything went blank and he could hear nothing at all. At his feet, the fluorescent lamp wobbled and toppled over. Dust filled his nostrils and coated his mouth.

He doubled up, pressing his forehead to the ground. He had tried to push the sound away as he had managed to push away the smell of blood, but he had failed. The noise of the explosion had been too much for his heightened senses. It was as if his skull were being crushed in a vice. He didn't care about anything now; couldn't think about Mum or Isabel. It didn't matter that Thorn was coming or that Pierce and Cain might escape with *Kronos*. In that moment – right *then* – Ash wanted nothing more than to die.

He felt Isabel put an arm around his shoulder and hold him, leaning her head against his and giving him a gentle shake.

Ash remained still, face contorted, as the pain began to subside.

Isabel shook him again, making him turn to look at her, and he realized she was speaking to him.

He watched her, seeing her lips move, but hearing nothing. Instead, he felt a cold fear wash over him. Goosebumps tingled down his back and across his scalp, popping to the surface of his skin like tiny explosions.

He couldn't hear.

In panic, he put his fingers into his ears and waggled them.

Isabel spoke again, deep concern in her expression as Ash took his fingers from his ears and looked at the blood smeared across them.

'I can't hear.' He held his hands out for Isabel to see the blood. '*I can't hear.*'

Isabel slung the satchel over her back, grabbed the light and took hold of Ash, pulling him along the corridor.

Ash stumbled along behind her in a daze, shaking his head, trying to banish the pain from his ears. His joints hurt too, and his muscles were aching, but as they moved along the corridor he began to feel better, and by the time they pushed through the doors at the end of the passage he actually felt *strong*. The pain in his head had faded to a dull throb and his joints felt smooth and efficient – but his hearing was still shot. The world was silent and dead around him.

Isabel led him into air that was grey and thick with dirt. The glow from the fluorescent tube diffused around them like they were drifting through dense winter fog, the particles moving about in a cloud. Swirls of it formed here and there like tiny whirlpools, then broke away and dissolved into nothing.

Isabel looked at Ash, her lips moving. He still couldn't make out what she was saying, but could detect a faint sound like the rushing of air. He shook his head at her. 'My ears feel weird.' They had started to itch somewhere deep inside. 'I think maybe I can hear something but . . . I don't know. It feels weird. Like . . . like something trying to get out. Or—'

Isabel gripped his arm and made him follow her down the stairs, turning the corner at the bottom of the first flight and coming to a dead stop.

It was a no-man's-land of destruction.

The lobby was awash with sunlight streaming through a large hole in the shutters, right behind the place where

Isabel had stuck the HEX13 onto the glass doors. Abou[t] the size of a small window, it was large enough for them to squeeze through. There was something else about the explosion that made Ash stop, though. Something that was going to make it impossible for him to escape – what lay between the stairs and the hole meant that the lobby might as well have been planted with land mines and barbed wire.

The counter behind which they had hidden from Thorn had been blown into splinters with such ferocity that the only part left standing was the far corner. It leant at a severe angle as if giant hands had torn it out of the ground, twisted it and tossed it aside. The computers were nothing but dust and smoke, and pieces of scorched paper were scattered on the ground, shuffling here and there. Embers danced like fireflies in the breeze. The glass doors and panes around the blast area were smashed into a thousand pieces, leaving jagged lightning bolts where there had once been smooth surfaces. Large spears of glass hung like gleaming icicles from the ceiling, ready to fall at any moment, and Ash knew that if they tried to cross the lobby, those shards could drop around them like a death trap.

The worst thing, though, was that all those splinters of wood and knives of broken glass were scattered every-where. There wasn't a clear patch between the stairs and the hole ripped through the shutters. Ash looked across at that sea of destruction, then down at his bare feet, and something became clear to him. 'It'll cut me to pieces.' His words sounded odd in his muffled ears. 'I'll never get across.'

Isabel stepped forward, moving down the stairs. Before she reached the bottom, though, she was walking on glass, and even in her heavy boots she had to tread carefully. An upturned shard could pierce the thick sole and slice through her skin without much pressure, and the slightest disturbance might cause any one of the overhead spears to fall.

When she stopped and looked back to say something, Ash shook his head and tapped one ear. 'I think it's getting better, but I still can't hear you.' It made him feel good that the damage to his ears obviously wasn't permanent. It gave him a new boost of hope, and he began to feel more positive. There had to be a way to get across.

'Wait,' he said. 'I've got a plan.' He heard his own voice, warped and fuzzy, as if it were coming to him down a long tunnel. 'See if you can find me a couple of pieces of wood from the counter. They need to be about this long.' He held his hands about thirty centimetres apart. 'And about this wide.' He narrowed the gap to fifteen centimetres.

Isabel looked at him in confusion before it dawned on her what he was planning. Her face lit up and she moved carefully over to the remains of the counter. Alternating between glancing up at the giant shards hanging from the ceiling, and scanning the ground, she searched left and right for what Ash needed, then crouched and held up a stumpy piece of dark wood.

Ash gave her a thumbs up.

It didn't take Isabel long to find another piece the right size, and then she was coming back, holding one in each hand.

By the time she reached him, Ash was sitting on the top step in just his pyjama bottoms. The sunlight streaming through the hole in the shutters highlighted his ribs beneath his skin as he took the pyjama shirt and ripped it down the middle. When that was done, he folded half the shirt into a long strip and placed it on the step. He took one of the pieces of wood, laid it on top of the strip, then rested his left foot on top of that. When he pulled up the ends of the material, they were like the ends of a giant, fat shoelace that he wrapped around once more and tied together before lifting his foot to test it.

'It'll do.'

He did the same with the other pieces of pyjama and wood, and within a couple of minutes he had a makeshift pair of shoes. It wasn't easy to walk in them, but he hobbled down the stairs and into the lobby, crunching glass under his weight. The pieces of wood stayed on his feet and the cotton held tight.

Isabel went ahead to the hole in the shutters and looked out, but as she did so, something moved above, drawing her attention. Her eyes widened in horror and she waved her hands at Ash, making him look up in time to see a spear of glass coming loose right over his head. It was at least as long as his arm, with a dagger-like point.

Just like in the storeroom, time dropped into treacle-like slow motion. Ash saw the huge piece of glass sway, then slip from the ceiling and begin to fall as if it were on film, being played a few frames at a time. He watched the glass spear drop past him as he took two large steps to the side before it smashed into the ground with a muffled crash. Above him other shards were coming loose. Like a complicated design of dominoes built to fall one after another, each shard of glass dislodged the next. A second slipped from a spot close to the first, and then a third and a fourth so that a nightmare of sharp death began to fall around him, showering him with splinters as they smashed into the floor.

'*Run!*' Isabel mouthed, but Ash was already moving faster than ever, running as if through a dream, stiff-legged because of the strange shoes.

He passed among the shards, anticipating which would fall next, flowing like water, twisting and dodging. One large piece came right at him, but he leant away and it whispered past, hitting the ground and exploding into a thousand pieces. Another just missed his toes as he turned his foot at the last moment – the glass cut like a razor through the cotton binding of the makeshift shoe. Without the material to keep it tight, the piece of wood slipped to one side, threatening to come loose.

Isabel was already climbing through the hole in the shutters. She threw the satchel into the clearing and followed it out head first. For a moment, all that was visible were her legs disappearing through the opening, and then she was gone.

The board on Ash's foot was loosening with each step, and the glass rain was cascading around him like it was never going to stop. Any moment now he expected to feel a sharp pain as something hit him in the head, or sliced through his back to pin him to the floor.

When the cotton finally ripped away, though, when the piece of wood finally slipped from his foot, leaving it naked to the terrible ground beneath, all he needed was one more step.

Just one.

It was the most painful step Ash had ever taken. He trod as lightly as he could, but when the glass cut through his skin, it was like fire enveloping his foot. He gritted his teeth and pushed down, launching himself head first at the hole in the metal shutters.

Arms stretched in front of him like he was diving into a swimming pool, Ash burst into the sunlight. As soon as his fingers touched the grass, he tucked in his head and tried to roll, but was moving faster than he realized. Instead, he landed in an undignified heap, his legs flipping over so he came down hard on his shoulder and landed on his back.

It didn't matter, though. He was out.

22 hrs and 02 mins until Shut-Down

Ash stared up, seeing not darkness, and not the blank walls of the research facility, but the expanse of a huge blue midday sky, dotted here and there with only the slightest wisp of cloud. He saw the endless greens of the trees and smelt the life around him, but couldn't enjoy any of it because his shoulders were aching from the fall and his foot was in agony from the cuts.

'*¡Increíble!*' Isabel said. 'You moved so fast. How did you do that? I've never seen . . . *Madre de Dios*, you're bleeding.'

'Mmm.' Ash sat up and squinted against the sun to see her.

'Are you OK?'

'I think so.'

'And you can hear me?'

Ash looked at Isabel and blinked in surprise. 'Yeah. I can. That's weird. I can hear fine.'

'And you moved so fast. How did you do that?'

'I don't know, I just . . . It doesn't make sense. A few minutes ago, I was deaf and now . . .' Ash turned his head this way and that, listening to his surroundings, picking up the chirrup of insects, the birds in the canopy, the distant grunt of something hiding in the forest. If anything, his hearing was even *better* than before. He could pinpoint a sound and focus on it with more control and less effort.

He sat up further and grabbed his foot, holding it with both hands and twisting so he could see the sole. There was blood all over it, and when he wiped it away more oozed from several large cuts.

'It looks bad,' Isabel said. 'Can you walk?'

Ash winced as he picked out the glass. It hurt like hell, but he didn't want to tell Isabel that. She was tough and he wanted to be tough too. 'I'll be fine.' He removed the binding from his other foot and stood up. Pain shot through him in sickening waves. Trying to take his mind off it, he looked over at the helicopter lying crumpled at the far edge of the clearing. 'We should check that out.'

'I think they didn't survive.' Isabel turned away, not wanting to see the broken vehicle.

'You don't know that. They *might* have survived. And if we're going to catch Cain and Pierce, we'll need some help. Maybe they've got supplies we can use. You know, a first-aid kit or something?'

All around, the forest was alive with alien sounds; whistles and calls and creaks and chirps. The whole place hummed, like it was singing its own song. There was movement too. Everywhere Ash looked there was something to draw his eye, and he had to control it the way he controlled what he listened to and what he could smell. It was as if he had to learn to use his senses in a different way, trying not to be distracted by everything.

Limping closer to the helicopter, he sniffed the air, tasting aviation fuel, burning electrics and the hint of blood lying beneath it. He allowed himself to hear the gentle sounds of ticking, the quiet groan of metal expanding and settling into place under the heat of the sun.

'It didn't catch fire,' he said. 'Maybe they got out.' Every helicopter he'd ever seen crash in a film had exploded in a ball of fire, so maybe this crash hadn't been so bad. Maybe the pilot had escaped.

He picked his way around the wreck, studying the helicopter as if it were a felled beast. The tail boom was lying close to the tree it had hit, tangled with what was left of the electric fence. It occurred to Ash that whatever they had been trying to keep out would now find it easy to get inside the compound.

Though he had detected the scent of blood, he still held out some hope for the pilot and his friend, but when he approached he knew it was a lost cause. The crumpled fuselage lay on its side, and both men were dead. They were still held in by their seat belts, but they were slumped with arms hanging loose, and their faces were unrecogniz-able. The cockpit was a mess of twisted metal, broken plastic and blood. Smoke drifted from the controls – and Ash realized immediately that anything useful on board would have been destroyed.

'Well?' Isabel called.

Ash shook his head and looked into the trees.

'And the radio?'

He shook his head again.

'We must go after them ourselves, yes?'

'Yes.' Ash walked away from the useless helicopter. The pain in his foot was subsiding now, weakening to a dull throb.

'No one to help us,' Isabel said.

'No one to help us,' he agreed.

'I've been in there many times,' Isabel said. 'The jungle. With Papa, and sometimes on my own. It is very dangerous, but I know the island. We will reach the boat and we will get the cure. First we need to be . . . How you say? "*Preparado*."

'Prepared?'

'*Sí.* We go to my house first. Quickly.'

From behind, Ash heard a muffled *CRUMP!* and he looked back at the hole in the BioSphere they had emerged from a few minutes ago. 'You hear that?'

'I don't hear so good as you.'

'I think it's Thorn. He must have got the HEX13 – figured out how to use it. He's coming.'

'Then we must get what we need and go,' Isabel replied. 'He won't find us in the jungle.'

21 hrs and 42 mins until Shut-Down

There was a narrow path cut into the forest, lined with fencing that was still intact, creating a corral for them to hurry along. Thick roots protruded from the compacted earth and new shoots broke the black dirt in places where the forest tried to reclaim what had once been its own. The hard ground was cruel to Ash's feet after the soft grass of the clearing.

'It's hot.' Isabel wiped a hand across her forehead.

'I thought it would be hotter.' Ash wondered if this was another strange effect the island was having on him. When he had first emerged into the clearing, before the helicopter crash and the shooting, he had felt the heat, but now he wasn't much warmer or colder than when he was inside the

BioSphere. His other senses had gone haywire, so why not this one too?

They followed the path for no more than five minutes before they came out into a second grassy clearing. This one was smaller and still surrounded by a high fence, but instead of a single large building of glass and metal this area was occupied by four comfortable-looking houses. Each one was a bungalow built to the same design, with a veranda and low wall running right around it. The roofs were tiled black, the woodwork painted dark green, and there were hanging baskets below the eaves, trailing bursts of flowers in the most amazing reds and yellows and whites. There were plants around each house, overgrown gardens that boasted mango trees, coconut palms and banana plants.

'This is where you live?' It was hard for Ash to believe that not long ago he had been standing in his bedroom looking out at a grey autumn evening in England. This wasn't just another country; it was another world.

Isabel carried on into the clearing, marching like a soldier. She went straight to the first house, passing between a pair of laden banana plants, and climbed the green-painted concrete steps onto the veranda. The mosquito-netted screen door creaked when she pushed on it and hurried into the house. Ash followed.

'You need clothes,' Isabel said, leading them through the sitting room. 'And boots. I'll find you something.' There was a rattan sofa with yellow cushions, two matching armchairs and a glass-topped table. A dark wooden bookshelf stood at the far end, heavy with paperbacks.

The black and white checked tiles were cool on Ash's feet as he followed Isabel through an arch into the dining room, leaving bloody footprints in his wake. From there, three doors opened into other rooms, and there was a screen door at the end, leading back outside. Isabel marched through to the right and into what Ash guessed was her bedroom.

It was a good size, with posters of film stars and rock bands covering the walls, and for some reason that surprised Ash. In some ways, it was just like his own bedroom at home – filled with books and CDs and the kind of knick-knacks that made it personal. There were a few soft toys and cushions on the bed, a chest of drawers topped with framed photos and pots of different flavours of lip balm, and a noticeboard with notes and pictures pinned to it. However, as well as all the usual stuff Ash would have expected in a girl's bedroom, there was also a rifle hanging on the wall and a large survival knife lying on the bedside table.

'Try these.' Isabel yanked open the wardrobe and pulled out a pair of her trousers. She threw them to him, and he just managed to catch them before they hit him in the face.

Ash held up the trousers and glanced round the room. 'Umm . . .'

'I won't look.' She tutted and stuck her head back in the wardrobe, continuing to rummage. 'I don't want to see.'

Ash turned around and slipped out of his pyjama bottoms, pulling on the trousers as quickly as he could.

They belonged to Isabel, so were a little too long, and he rolled them up before looking back to see Isabel holding out a plain black T-shirt in one hand and a pair of boots in the other.

'You must clean your feet,' she said as Ash took them from her.

She didn't wait to see if they fit him, but went into the adjoining bathroom and switched on the shower. 'In the forest it is hot and wet. The cuts will get . . . how you say? Infected.'

Infected. Ash shivered at the word, and pulled on the T-shirt. It was a good fit, and felt snug around his chest and shoulders.

'Clean them,' Isabel said, and hurried off to find a first-aid box while Ash went into the bathroom and stuck his feet under the shower, washing away the blood and dirt.

When they were clean, he inspected the wounds, finding them to be smaller than before. The pain had been terrible and there had been a good deal of blood, but looking at them now they weren't much more than bad scratches. He dried them with a towel, then glanced up at himself in the mirror over the sink.

That was when he remembered what Isabel had said when they first met. Something about his hair. He had been confused at the time, but hadn't given it another thought until now, so he scraped it all flat against his head and leant closer to inspect it. Instead of being completely black, there was now a faint streak of white, just left of centre and about two centimetres wide, running from the crown at the back of his head, all the way to the front.

He leant closer still, putting a hand to the hair and lifting it, wondering how it could have happened, but when he looked himself in the eyes, he received an even bigger surprise.

Instead of dark brown, his eyes were now green.

'What's happening to me?' he said, looking at Isabel's reflection when she returned holding a first-aid kit. 'What's going on?'

'What do you mean?'

'I . . .' He didn't quite know how to tell her. 'My eyes . . . they're a different colour.'

'They can't be.'

'Two days ago they were brown.'

Isabel frowned and wiped a bead of sweat from her brow. 'It must be the light. Sometimes it makes things look different.'

'But they look *so* different. And what about my hair? It wasn't . . . I mean, where did *this* come from?' Ash pointed to the white streak. 'It's supposed to be black.'

Isabel came forward and placed the first-aid kit on the edge of the sink. She looked exhausted, and her face was glistening with sweat. 'I once heard about someone whose hair went white after an accident. It was stress, I think.'

'What? Just like that?'

Isabel put out a hand to touch the white streak. 'It looks cool.'

'Will it all go like that? All of my hair?'

'I don't know.'

'But it did for the person you heard about?'

'I guess.'

Ash continued to stare at it. 'But it's so . . . perfect. Like a perfect streak. The same all the way along. And that's not the only thing.' He tore himself away from the mirror and sat down on the toilet, turning his foot for Isabel to see. 'Look at this.'

'They don't look too bad,' Isabel said.

'Exactly. But it felt so much worse. And I'm sure when I looked at them before, the cuts were bigger.'

'Bigger how?'

Ash looked up at Isabel. 'Something strange is happening to me. I can hear better than before, smell things I couldn't smell before. I can even see better. I *look* different, I feel stronger, and now it's like . . . I dunno, like my feet are healing faster than they should.'

Isabel shook her head as if she didn't understand.

'There's something here,' Ash said. 'Something in the BioSphere, or something on this island, that's changing me. There has to be; I can *feel* it.'

'It hasn't changed *me*. I think maybe . . . maybe you're—'

'I'm not imagining it,' Ash said. 'Don't tell me I'm imagining it.'

'I wasn't going to—'

'This place is for research, right? Well, maybe there's some kind of weird research going on; something in the air. Maybe that's what's happening to me.'

'I don't know.' Isabel shrugged. 'I can't explain.'

'Pierce said this was the Devil's island, that there's stuff out there . . . Maybe there's something going on here that you don't know about.'

Isabel sighed. 'Well, this island is different, yes, but not the people.'

'Different how?'

'The plants. And the animals.'

'How are they different?' Ash noticed that Isabel's eyes were a little bloodshot, and her face was drained of colour.

'It takes too long to explain. It is best to see for yourself.' She opened the first-aid kit and handed him a bandage and a tube of antiseptic cream. 'Finish fixing your feet.' She placed another two bandages on the floor beside him. 'And when you're done, wrap these around your boots. You will leave not so many prints in the ground. It will make us more difficult to follow.'

'Are you all right?' Ash had been so preoccupied with himself that he hadn't thought to ask. 'You look tired.'

'It's been a hard day.' Isabel raised her eyebrows.

'Yeah. I guess it has.' But Ash watched her for a moment longer, seeing how hot and exhausted she looked. *He* had almost never felt stronger or fitter than he did right then, but Isabel looked terrible. And she had a new smell about her. The same thing he had detected when they first entered the lab area of the BioSphere: the odour of unburnt cooker gas.

The sneering voice in his head spoke again, but this time it only had one word to say to him:

Kronos.

They didn't stay in the house for any longer than necessary.

Isabel grabbed what they needed and stuffed some of it into the satchel they had taken from the storage facility. She jammed the rest into a small rucksack that she threw over her back, then pulled her hair back into a ponytail.

'You carry this.' She gave the satchel to Ash. 'And take this.' She handed him a thick belt. 'You don't go out there without one.'

Ash took the belt from her and buckled it round his waist before pulling the knife from the sheath attached to it. It was the same as the one now hanging from Isabel's belt – with a black rubberized grip and a dark blade that looked huge in his small hand. It was serrated near the hilt, tapering to an upturned point. On the front of the sheath, there was a pocket containing a fire steel.

Isabel turned and bustled towards the back door and Ash was about to put the knife away when he had an idea. He touched the blade against the edge of his palm and drew it across the skin in one quick, short motion. The razor-sharp steel sliced a shallow cut and beads of dark red blood welled up.

'Come on,' Isabel called.

Ash shoved the knife back into its sheath and fastened the Velcro. He put the cut to his mouth, sucking away the blood, then followed Isabel out the back and let the screen door slam behind him.

'He won't find us in the forest,' Isabel said as they passed the other houses, jogging across the grass towards the far edge of the clearing.

Ash was grateful for Isabel's spare boots, even if they

weren't a good fit. With two pairs of socks and the band-ages, though, they were snug, so his feet didn't bother him as he ran. Over his shoulder, the satchel bounced against his back. 'How will *we* find *them*, though?' he asked. 'Cain and Pierce?'

'I know this forest.' Isabel sounded out of breath already. 'We'll find them or get to the boat first.'

'Then what? We have to get *Zeus* – the antiviral your dad told us about. The cure.'

'I know that,' Isabel said. 'I just don't know *how*.'

'We'll think of something,' he said, as much to persuade himself as Isabel.

'Yeah.'

'Is that yours?' Ash pointed at the rifle she was carrying. She had taken it from the rack on her bedroom wall as they were leaving. 'Is it real?'

'No, it's a toy.'

'So why did—'

'*Duh.* Of course it's real,' Isabel said.

'Could you . . . could you kill someone with it?'

'Easily.' Isabel reached the door in the fence at the far edge of the compound and came to a stop. 'Look.' She crouched and pointed at a footprint in the soft ground close to a large root. 'They must have followed the track out here. They came this way.'

'You sure?'

'Of course.' Isabel stood and unlatched the gate. She turned to Ash with a serious expression. 'When we go into the forest, you must do as I say. Go where I go. Step where

I step. Don't touch anything. Don't leave any trail for Thorn to follow. Always look before you sit. There are many dangerous things in there. Easy to get hurt, easy to get lost.'

'All right.' Ash nodded. 'I've been in a jungle before and—'

'This jungle is different. Do not touch anything. Step where I step.'

'OK. I understand.'

'And the forest is not like the BioSphere,' Isabel said. 'In there we had Thorn. In here' – she pointed at the trees – 'we have Thorn *and* everything else.'

21 hrs and 03 mins until Shut-Down

They had been in the forest less than half an hour and already it was like they were a million miles from the rest of the world. There was nothing but trees, heat and the thick, musky smell of damp earth and decaying leaves. And when Ash tested the air, he could pick out all kinds of unusual scents he didn't recognize.

Ahead and behind them, the forest hummed with the sound of cicadas and the call of unseen birds, but immediately around them was a cocoon of silence as everything lay still, waiting for them to pass.

Ash had been in a jungle in India, with Dad, and thought he knew what to expect, but this was different. Isabel had been right when she said he would have to see it for himself, because it would have been hard for her to explain the uncomfortable feeling he experienced the deeper they travelled into the forest. The further they went, the more it was as if he were being watched. It was a similar feeling to the one he'd had when they were in the dark of the Bio-Sphere. He could hear things moving about in the treetops, and in the thick jungle around them, but whatever was out there sensed when he focused on it, and fell silent and still.

And then there were those insects. Ash had seen enough mosquitoes to know what they were, but instead of being tiny, these were as big as his fingernail, with black and white striped bodies and spindly legs hanging beneath them. Isabel told Ash to spread dirt on his face to keep them from biting him, so now they were both painted with dry mud. As far as he could tell, none of them had yet bitten him, but already a few bumps had formed on Isabel's face.

Isabel moved through the jungle like it was second nature to her. She warned Ash whenever they came across something dangerous – trees covered with spikes like six-inch nails, others with tiny hairs that could pierce the skin like splinters and cause weeks of itching. He saw a bright red caterpillar as fat as his thumb, bristling with long spines that Isabel told him could give him a terrible rash. He spotted a huge praying mantis perched on a low hanging branch, eyes twitching, and Isabel pointed out something the size of a rat scuttling beneath the leaves at her feet.

'Scorpion spider,' she said. 'Not poisonous, but it can bite. Most places they like the dark, but here . . .' She shrugged. 'Here, it is different.'

'Scorpion spider?' Ash watched the spot where it had disappeared into the trees. 'But it's massive. And who thought *that* was a good idea? A cross between a scorpion and a spider?'

'You like that, you will love this.' Isabel nodded towards a huge web strung between two trees. In the centre of it sat a yellow narrow-bodied spider with a leg span that was wide enough to cover the top of Ash's head.

Ash shuddered.

'I see what you mean about this place,' he said. 'There's something not right about it.'

'Now you understand?'

'Yeah. Everything looks a bit bigger. I mean, the trees are enormous, so *high*, and the bugs . . .' He shivered. 'Is it something to do with the BioSphere?'

'Papa says *Isla Negra* was a place for research for many years. Not just the BioSphere, but also before. He thinks maybe something escaped.'

'Something like what?' Ash looked around, trying to see what was hiding in the trees.

'Not monsters,' said Isabel. 'Bugs. Very small. In the air.'

'You mean like bacteria and stuff?'

'Yes. Or maybe animals used for research. He has been trying to find out what made it happen.'

'And he hasn't figured it out yet?'

'No.'

Ash wondered if that was why he felt different. Maybe it was something to do with the air. But if that was true, then why didn't it have the same effect on Isabel?

'There's some really bad smells too,' Ash said. 'I can smell something ahead that's dis*gusting*. It's like there must be a gigantic dog in here somewhere and it's just done a massive poo.' He shook his head and banished the smell, focusing on something else.

'I don't smell it.'

'Well, if we keep going in this direction, I have a feeling you will.'

Sure enough, the deeper they went into the jungle, the stronger it became until eventually Isabel looked back at Ash. 'I smell it now. But only *just* now.'

Ash shrugged and they kept on going a few more metres until they came upon a brown fleshy plant the size of a football. It was split so that it opened like a giant mouth, and was red inside. Around the lips there were hundreds of white tendrils that, from a distance, looked like teeth. The smell that it gave off was worse than dog mess, and it made both of them gag as they hurried past.

From time to time Isabel stopped and pointed out a footprint, or a place where the foliage was damaged. 'They came this way,' she would say. 'See how they broke this branch?' Or she would mutter to herself, 'They are clumsy. Such a trail.'

Ash was concerned that he was also leaving an obvious trail, and watched Isabel closely. He did as she told him, avoiding what she avoided, stepping where she stepped, touching what she touched. As they progressed through the forest, he began to feel more at ease, like when Dad had taken him into the jungle in India.

After another half hour or so of trekking, Isabel stopped and crouched to examine the trail left by Pierce and the others. 'They went *that* way.' She pointed straight ahead, then stood and adjusted the pack she was carrying. She looked to her left, where the jungle was thicker. '*We* go this way.'

'What? Why not that way? Why not follow them?'

'We need to get ahead. This way is more difficult, but it's quicker. And Thorn will follow *their* prints instead of coming after us.'

Ash looked back to see that their bandage-wrapped boots had hardly left any prints, even in the soft ground. If they moved carefully – if Ash didn't leave a trail like a rampaging elephant – then Pierce and Cain's trail would be the more obvious route to follow. Isabel's idea made sense, but Ash still didn't like the thought of losing the trail, and he also wasn't so sure that taking a more difficult route would be a good idea, because Isabel looked exhausted.

'What if they're just up ahead?' he asked. 'They might be really close.'

'They are slow because they carry the crate, but they set off more than three hours ahead of us. Trust me. If we go this way we can still catch up.'

'Do you actually know where we're going?'

Isabel looked at Ash as if he had insulted her. 'Of course I know. The bay is at the north end of the island.' She brushed hair from her eyes. There were beads of sweat on her upper lip and on her forehead. She fished a compass from her pocket and turned it until the needle was aligned with the red *N*, then moved her finger in the direction it was indicating – towards the thicker trees. 'North.'

'You've been there before?'

'Yes.' She shoved the compass back into her pocket and adjusted the rifle slung over her shoulder.

'How long will it take?'

'I think maybe we arrive tomorrow.'

'*Tomorrow?*'

'I know.' She sighed. 'We don't have much time.' She looked up at the snatches of sunlight visible through the treetops. 'But when dark comes we will have to stop – for a while at least. It is more dangerous at night.'

Ash ran a hand over his head and looked at Isabel. The colour had drained from her skin. 'Are you feeling OK?'

'I'm fine.'

'We will catch up with them, won't we?'

She didn't answer.

'Say we will.'

Isabel blinked hard, as if she just wanted to close her eyes and go to sleep. When she opened them again, she looked at Ash. 'We will. We must be moving faster than they are, so we are catching them up all the time. And they will have to stop at night too.'

'But *Kronos* won't.' Ash couldn't stop thinking about Mum, locked in the lab, slowly dying. '*Kronos* won't stop at night.'

Isabel pursed her lips and shook her head. 'No.' She rubbed her face with both hands and when she took them away, her eyes were red. This was the first time since coming into the jungle that Ash had seen her so scared. She was growing weaker and becoming breathless, while he only felt stronger. He was worried about her, but he already had the burden of so many other things on his mind, he didn't want to think about losing Isabel's strength to prop him up. He needed her and had to believe she would be OK.

'So we're going to have to spend the night out here?' He changed the subject and looked at the plants growing tight around them. For one moment, he wondered if they were closer than they had been a minute ago. He had never seen plants move before, but in this place almost anything seemed possible.

'I know somewhere safe to stop.' Isabel sniffed. 'And we will leave as soon as it is light enough. Or maybe if there is a good moon we can risk moving at night. We'll have to wait and see.'

Ash was suddenly overcome with a sense of how lucky he was to have her. On his own, he would never have come this far; would never survive the jungle. 'I'm glad you're here,' he said.

Isabel nodded and started to smile.

'I mean, I should be thanking you. For getting us out of that place, for the clothes . . . everything. *Gracias.* Isn't that how you say "thank you" in Spanish?'

'*De nada,*' Isabel replied. 'You're welcome.'

'It doesn't seem real, does it? I mean . . . any of this.'

Isabel remained silent.

'I always thought Mum had a boring job, working in a lab,

but she was making a cure for some horrible disease. She was saving the world and I thought she was just some boring person in a white coat.'

Isabel pulled a water bottle from her rucksack. She unscrewed the cap and took a swig. 'What you said about being glad I'm here?'

'Mm-hm?'

'Well, I'm glad you're here too.' She held the bottle out to him. 'Drink. We need to stay strong.'

The water was warm and tasted tinny, but Ash hadn't realized how thirsty he was. The last time he'd had anything to drink was when he had woken up in the white room, and he had *no* idea when he'd last eaten. As if to confirm it had been a long time, his stomach let out a long grumble.

When they set off again, Isabel plucked a hand of bananas from a plant and passed one back to Ash.

'You sure they're safe to eat? Nothing weird about them?'

'They're safe. Just don't drop the skin where we walk. Leave no trail for Thorn.'

'But he'll follow the others, won't he?' Ash stripped back the bright yellow peel.

Isabel shrugged. 'I hope so.'

The fruit was small and sweet with flavour that exploded in his mouth. It was a lot better than the dry, bland bananas Mum got from the supermarket, and Ash didn't know whether that was because the fruit was different or because *he* was different. Either way, it didn't matter because he was starving, so he ate the first one in a couple of gulps and tossed the skin into the trees where it couldn't be seen, then took another.

'Don't eat too many.' Isabel warned. 'You'll get . . . how you say? Runny toilet.'

Ash couldn't help smiling. 'You mean the squirts.'

'The squirts,' Isabel said, making Ash burst out laughing.

'Is this funny? The squirts?'

'Yeah. Yeah, it's funny.'

Isabel raised her eyebrows and looked at her watch. 'It's just gone one thirty. We need to keep moving for another three or four hours – that should be just enough time to get to shelter before dark. It will be safe to stay there.'

20 hrs and 02 mins until Shut-Down

The jungle closed in on them, the trees growing so close and dense that the canopy became a solid ceiling. Shards of light pierced through in places and cut into the gloom, illuminating a faint mist that hung at ankle level, shimmering with an eerie glow. Vines twisted between trunks that bristled with spines and barbs, forming impenetrable maze-like walls. Unseen creatures grunted and moved in the shadows. Monstrous insects clung to distorted branches. A rich earthy smell hardly masked more sinister smells, and Ash found himself constantly on edge, testing everything, using all his senses to scan for danger.

At least twenty minutes since their last stop, they hacked their way through a thick tangle of vines to find themselves in a more open part of the jungle. There was a small area of hard, black dirt a few metres wide, with only one or two trees growing there. The ground was punctuated with smooth stones and small patches of ferns. On the far side, the jungle was more evenly spaced, easier to travel through, so they paused to rest before moving on. The sweet smell of freshly spilt sap was still in the air and, above them, a shaft of sunlight broke through the canopy.

Ash studied his friend as she drank from the water bottle. He noticed her discomfort when she swallowed, and saw a sudden shiver wrack her body. He could tell that something was making her feel unwell, but she hadn't said anything. She hadn't complained even once.

Seeing her like that made him realize he had been trying to ignore a nasty idea that was simmering in his thoughts. As he watched Isabel, though, the idea began to form so quickly that he couldn't stop it. It gained weight and settled over his already aching heart: Mum was wrong about the virus being contained.

That was the scent Ash had detected when he entered the lab area.

The smell of unburnt cooker gas was *Kronos*.

And that's why it was all over Isabel – because it had escaped and was now working its way through her blood.

He was sure of it. But he couldn't understand why it wasn't affecting him. As he struggled with his thoughts, a feral sound came from somewhere out of sight. He had heard something like it earlier, but said nothing because it was far away, but this time it was much closer.

'There's something out there.' He became more alert, switching his focus away from Isabel.

'Where?' Isabel screwed the cap back onto the water bottle and looked about, trying to listen.

'There.' Ash pointed to their left, through the hole they had hacked in the vines. 'It sounds big.'

'Thorn?'

Ash shook his head and got to his feet, slinging the satchel over his shoulder. 'It's coming this way. Right towards us. I think we should go.'

'What is it?' Isabel stood up beside him and raised her rifle.

'I don't know.' Ash started walking backwards, keeping his eyes on the gap in the vines. 'But it's moving faster.'

'OK. This way.' Isabel grabbed her backpack and secured it, then pushed ahead. 'Let me go first.'

'Fine, but just hurry up.'

They ran to the other side of the small clearing and forged on into forest. Isabel still couldn't hear anything, but Ash could hear it as plain as if it were right beside him. Something big and clumsy was crashing through the thick jungle in their wake, and whatever it was, it wasn't being anywhere near as careful as they had been; it was blundering through, smashing things out of its way. It must have been strong, thick-skinned, and knew the jungle well – there was no way Ash and Isabel would have been able to travel through that area so quickly and avoid all the barbs and spines. At that speed, they would have been ripped to shreds.

'It's getting closer.' Ash couldn't help the way his voice tightened in his throat. 'Hurry up.'

'We can't go any faster,' Isabel panted. 'Not here.' They were coming to another area of dense growth, the trees closing in on them once more. Some of the thick trunks had spines as long as pencils and as sharp as hypodermic needles. A simple misstep, an accidental trip, and those spines would slide through their flesh as if through butter.

Behind them, the noise grew louder, like an approaching freight train forcing its way through the forest. Ash could hear the foliage being rammed aside, the snap and crack of branches breaking. 'Quick!'

It was *so close* now. Something huge and unstoppable.

'We can't!' Isabel shouted in frustration. 'The jungle is too thick.' She stopped and pulled the rifle from over her shoulder, pointing it into the forest behind them.

The crashing stopped.

Ash came to a halt and moved his head to listen. He sniffed the air, smelling something musty and unpleasant.

'Is it gone?' Isabel kept the rifle raised.

As Ash turned to look at her, he heard something. No more than twenty metres away. An animal-like grunt. There was a pause, then the crashing began again. 'It's coming. Let's get the hell out of here.'

But Isabel didn't move. She stayed as she was, rifle aimed into the forest as the thundering and smashing grew louder and louder. She stood her ground – even when the foliage split on the other side of the clearing and a monstrous creature burst into the open.

It straightened its front legs and came to a shuddering stop.

Slavering and grunting, the gigantic boar must have weighed at least three times as much as a grown man. On all fours, it was taller than Ash, but if it had reared onto its hind legs, it would have been two metres tall. Its wide, hunched shoulders were packed hard with solid muscle, supporting a huge, pointed head that tapered to a black nose as big as a dinner plate. A line of bristles stood up from the ridge of its sloping back, and it had short, powerful legs to support its massive bulk. Tusks stuck out from either side of its lower jaw like curved, razor-sharp blades more than thirty centimetres long. Ash knew that one thrust from those yellowed and dirty weapons would split him down the middle.

The beast stood there with thick saliva hanging from its jaws, its breathing slow and heavy, its chest expanding and relaxing. The smell that enveloped it was an intoxicating mix of rotting meat, sour milk and death.

'Shoot it,' Ash whispered.

Almost exactly as he said it, Isabel fired a warning shot.

CRACK!

The sudden noise was deafening in the confines of the close trees. The sound reverberated in Ash's head, and at the other side of the small clearing the beast flinched as Isabel's bullet struck the ground between its front legs.

Apart from that slight twitch, though, there was no indication that the creature was bothered. It didn't make a sound. It didn't move forwards or backwards. It simply stood where it was, head lowered, with its small dark eyes fixed on them. Only its nose moved, crinkling and twitching.

'Kill it.'

Isabel quickly worked the bolt on her rifle, loading another cartridge into the chamber. The spent one flicked out of the breech and sailed through the air in front of Ash. It caught the light, glittering like gold, then dropped to the floor and disappeared beneath the leaves. She steadied the rifle, taking aim once more between the boar's front legs.

CRACK!

The second bullet struck the ground in the same place as the first, but this time the animal didn't even flinch.

'*Shoot* it,' Ash whispered. '*Just kill it.*'

Isabel reloaded the rifle with a quick movement of the bolt, but as she looked down the barrel, preparing to put the next bullet into the creature's head, Ash realized that it was not looking at *them*.

It was looking at *him*.

Its small, black, marble-like eyes were fixed on *him*.

And as Ash returned the stare, the boar shifted its gaze. It looked once to its left, then to the right, as if it didn't know what to do. It snorted and lowered its head, then turned and trotted back into the forest.

Ash stared at the empty space where the monster had been.

Beside him, Isabel remained motionless with the rifle still aimed into the trees. 'It was you,' she said. 'It stopped because of you.'

Ash continued to look at the small grooves in the ground where the boar had skidded to a halt. 'You missed.'

'They don't see good, but it saw you. It smelt you.'

'You missed,' Ash said again, still staring.

'Yes. To scare it away. We don't kill things unless—'

'You *should* have killed it.'

'We don't kill anything. The animals on *Isla Negra* are like nowhere else. *Muy raro.* Very important.' She frowned. 'Like in the lab. You saw those monkeys there, right? But Papa tells me they only study them. Never kill.'

Ash blinked and looked at her. 'You've seen one of those things before?'

'*Sí.* Three times in the jungle. And one time there was one in the BioSphere – for study.'

'That's why there's an electric fence.' Ash was starting to understand now. 'To keep them out. Because they're dangerous.'

'They don't often come close.'

'What is *wrong* with this place?' Ash kicked the ferns at his feet, then shook his head and took a deep breath to calm himself. 'Look, next time you shoot it, OK? Promise me. I thought it was going to kill us.'

'Usually it works with the animals. A gunshot usually scares them—'

'*Promise* me.'

'OK. I promise.' Isabel held up her hand. 'But it saw you and stopped. Why did it do that? And then it walked away. What did you do?'

'I didn't do anything.'

Isabel clicked on the safety and lowered the rifle.

'Don't look at me like that,' Ash said.

'Like what?'

'Like . . . I'm weird or something.'

'You *are* weird.' Isabel stepped closer and put a hand on his arm. She squeezed it once and tried to smile. 'But you are still my friend.'

'So why didn't you tell me about those things?'

'I didn't want to scare you.'

'Is there anything *else* out here I should be scared of?'

'Yes.' Isabel slung the rifle over her shoulder. 'Lots of things. Come on. Thorn will have heard the shots.'

They fell into an uneasy silence as they moved on. So many things battled for thinking space inside Ash's head, and the boar attack had alerted him to even more of the dangers in the forest. He was sure the animal was bigger than it was supposed to be. It was bigger than any boar *he'd* ever heard of. He wanted to ask Isabel about it, but he couldn't stop thinking about the way she had looked at him – almost as if she were afraid of him – but *he* didn't know why the boar had stopped. He had no idea why it had turned and walked away. Perhaps it was the same reason why the mosquitoes didn't bite him, and the leaves of some plants curled up when he came close to them.

The most important thing, though, was to be alert for other boars, so he kept his ears tuned to the sound it had made, and had no difficulty remembering the smell it carried. He reassured himself that Isabel had the rifle, and was a good shot; she had planted two shots right between its legs, so he guessed she could have put one between its eyes if she wanted to. As she walked ahead of him, Ash watched the weapon bouncing against her back and thought about her promise. If they were attacked again, she would shoot to kill. It made him wonder though; what if it was a person who attacked them? Would she be prepared to shoot *then*?

As the day wore on, the sky began to darken and a low rumbling sounded in the distance.

Isabel stopped to look up. 'There's rain coming.'

Ash scanned the canopy, looking through a spot where the trees were thinner. The sky was grey now, instead of the wonderful blue it had been when they had escaped the BioSphere.

'Well.' She shrugged. 'It *is* the rainforest.'

Within minutes, the rain came down like nails. It hammered the leaves of the canopy and broke through to pound Ash and Isabel with huge drops that drenched them in seconds. The ground turned to black rivers of mud under their feet.

'At least it will cover our tracks,' Isabel shouted over the sound of the deluge.

They were climbing a steep bank, making their way towards the top of a hill, and it was becoming more and more difficult to walk. Their trousers were caked in mud, their boots heavy with it, and every step was an effort. Where they could, they clung to tree trunks and branches, helping to haul each other up, afraid they were going to slip and be washed right back down to the bottom.

At the top, they stopped to rest, but only for a few minutes. Cain might not rest. Thorn might not rest. They couldn't take the risk that one would get too far ahead, or the other would catch up, so they stopped just long enough for Isabel to catch her breath.

The trees were a little thinner up here, spaced further apart, and there were places where Ash could look across the forest at the sea of leaves being pounded by the storm. Sheets of rain drove down, and the jungle stretched on into the haze, rising as it clung to the slopes of low mountains whose craggy peaks burst free of the trees in the distance, and reached for the sky.

'It's amazing,' Ash said.

'You should see it when the sun is shining. Papa says there's nothing as beautiful. It is worth the danger of the forest just to see this.'

Ash looked at Isabel standing beside him, hair plastered to her face, drips beading in her eyelashes, clothes drenched and covered with mud.

'We'll save them,' he said, 'won't we?'

Isabel bit her lip and looked away. 'We should get moving.'

Ash was suddenly aware of the heat coming off her, of the increased rate of her heartbeat. The word *Kronos* drifted into his thoughts.

'At the bottom, we'll cross the river,' Isabel said. 'From there it's a short walk to the shelter. In good weather it wouldn't take long.'

'And in this rain?'

'I don't know. And maybe the river . . .' Isabel shook her head.

'Maybe the river what?' Ash asked.

'Nothing. Let's go.'

19 hrs and 15 mins until Shut-Down

Climbing the hill had been difficult, but the descent was harder. Every time Ash put his foot down, it either sank or slipped in the mud, and grabbing at the trees meant puncturing his hands on spiky branches or burning his skin as they whipped through his fingers.

Halfway down the slope, Isabel cut a long straight branch from a nearby tree and skinned the thorns from it. When it was smooth, she handed it to Ash before cutting another for herself. 'Walking stick,' she said. 'It might help.'

It didn't. He continued to slip and slide his way down as the rain battered them and the sky rumbled. Almost every speck of light had now gone, and the world had become a miserable, dirty place. Ash had been relieved to escape the

BioSphere, but now he wished he was back. At least it had been dry in there.

But he wasn't going to be beaten. He looked down the slope, unable to see the bottom because it was lost in the rain, and touched the identity tag around his neck. *The best survivors never give up* is what Dad had told him. *They stay positive and keep moving forward. That's why they survive.* Stay strong, stay positive, and keep moving forward. And as he stared at the slope, trying to lift his spirits, he remembered the park near their house. It had a steep bank that was great for sledging in the winter. Ash used to go there with Dad, each dragging a bright-red plastic sled. They would trudge to the top and race down, usually turning over and spilling into the snow. Sometimes they would run down, trying not to slip, and Ash had always thought it was easier to just run full pelt. It was more fun too.

Maybe that would work with mud.

Without giving himself a chance to back out, Ash dropped the stick, lifted his head and took off down the slope. He moved so quickly that his boots didn't even have time to sink or slip on the mud; he just kept going, rushing down, sidestepping the trees. He was like a crazed maniac, with the rain splashing in his face and his hair stuck to his scalp, but it felt fantastic.

For that moment, there was no *Kronos* or Thorn; there was no Mum, no Isabel. There was just Ash running down a muddy slope, muscles pumping, chest pounding, rain crashing around him. And unlike his clumsy runs down the snowy slopes at home, he was aware of everything. He could see the individual raindrops falling in slow motion before his eyes. He could sense the ground beneath his feet, and see the pattern of the bark on the trees. He could pick out the individual spines, the insects nestling in the knots. His breathing was regular, his legs were strong, he saw and heard and smelt everything. He was invincible. Unstoppable. Indestructible. He could not . . . slip.

His right foot skidded out from beneath him, shooting upwards, flipping him over onto his back. He landed hard and continued to slide along the torrent of mud flowing downhill, picking up speed as he went. The bubble of slow motion popped as Ash tried to dig his heels in, but they just swept through the soft ground. He floundered, grabbing at branches that were out of reach. Trees zipped past on either side and he knew he would crash into one at any moment, maybe breaking a leg or an arm, or both.

But it was worse than that. When he caught sight of the bottom of the slope, appearing out of the misty rain, Ash realized it didn't level out to a safe, flat area.

Several metres below his position, the slope came to an abrupt stop and then fell away to a sheer drop where there was nothing but space.

A cliff.

Ash twisted onto his front and dug his hands into the mud. He clawed at it, ripping his fingertips and cracking his nails as he started to slow down; but not enough.

The sound of rain crashed in his ears. Terror burnt through his veins. The edge came closer and closer, emptying into space beyond.

'No.' He frantically snatched at roots and trunks and branches. '*No!*'

And then his fingers closed around a sapling that bent with his weight and allowed him to grip it tight. His arm reached its full stretch, then yanked hard, pulling at his shoulder, bringing him to an abrupt stop. His legs whipped out over the cliff edge, touching nothing, and his heart lurched. If he loosened his grip, he would slip and be gone, falling into nothing.

Full of panic, he reached up with his other arm and grasped the sapling, hardly aware of how easily he dragged his full weight away from the edge. He pulled himself up and hugged the tree like a drowned rat clinging on for life.

The rain continued to pound him as he looked up the slope at Isabel's dark shape moving down through the trees. The noise of it filled his head, threatening to drive him mad, until another sound broke through. Something he hadn't expected to hear.

Isabel was bent over, laughing so hard she couldn't even talk.

'What's so funny?' Ash shouted, feeling his eyes sting. 'What's so funny?' His voice was hoarse, his throat sore. 'I could have died!'

Isabel continued to laugh, both hands on her stick that was now planted firmly in the ground, and in that moment Ash hated her with all his heart. He hated this place and he hated *everything*. All the fear and anger and confusion was rising up and boiling in him now. He'd had enough of being strong and positive. He wanted to hit something or break something or make someone pay for what had happened to him over the last few hours. He hadn't asked for any of it. He hadn't *wanted* any of it.

'Stop laughing!' he shouted. 'I could have died! I. Could. Have. *Died!*'

Isabel stopped and looked down at him, peering through sodden hair that had come loose from her ponytail and hung across her face. '*Lo siento.* I'm sorry.' She shifted, pulling her stick from the ground, and came to where Ash was kneeling. She eased down and sat in the mud beside him. 'Look.' She waved a hand towards the edge of the cliff. 'No one was going to die.'

Ash took a deep breath, then turned and sat beside her, still holding onto the sapling that had saved his life. He wiped the rain and tears from his eyes and squinted through the downpour at the edge of the cliff.

'It's not far to fall,' Isabel said. 'Three or four metres.'

From higher up, where Ash had first slipped, it had looked like he was sliding towards a cliff, but now he was closer he could see that he wouldn't have fallen far to the pebbled bank below. The bump would have hurt, but it wouldn't have been fatal. And beyond the short stretch of pebbles, Ash could see why he had thought the rain sounded so loud.

'The river looks dangerous,' Isabel said. 'The rain is making it fast.'

The water was raging round the bend to their left. It crashed against large black rocks at its edges, spraying white foam into the rain.

'I still could have got hurt,' Ash sulked. 'And I've got a thing about heights.'

'A thing?'

'You know, I'm . . . I don't like them.' It sounded ridiculous after everything they'd been through.

'You are scared of heights?'

'I don't *like* them. It's not the same thing.'

Isabel nodded as if she understood, but they both knew that not liking heights and being scared of them were exactly the same thing.

'I went to this place one time, for a friend's birthday party, and we had to climb around all these obstacles in the tree-tops. There were tightropes and cargo nets and it was really high up, and . . . well, I *really* didn't want to do it, but I didn't want to look like a wimp either. There was a zip wire from right at the top of this massive tree, and I just had to close my eyes and jump off the platform. About halfway down, the pulley jammed and . . .' Ash could remember it clearly – the sudden jolt, the bite of the harness cutting into his thighs, the tight fist of terror that crushed his insides. 'I got stuck. I was just dangling there for ages before they could get me down. All my friends thought it was funny. They were looking up at me and laughing, and all I could think was that the cable was going to snap and I was going to fall and die.' He looked at Isabel, thinking she was so much tougher than him. 'Pretty lame, huh? I bet you're not scared of anything.'

'Small dogs.' She wiped a drip of rainwater from the end of her nose.

'What?'

'Little dogs. I don't know why. They look scary when they move, I guess, and all that noise they make. I'm sorry, it was bad to laugh.'

Ash put his chin on his knees and watched the river boiling.

'Why did you run?' Isabel asked. 'The jungle is dangerous. You should do what I tell you.'

'Yeah. You said that.'

Isabel shuffled closer, so her shoulder was against his, then she nudged him. 'It was funny.'

Ash squirmed away and continued to look at the river.

Isabel moved closer and nudged him again. 'It really was.'

Ash thought about what he must have looked like, running off like an idiot, sliding down the bank. Isabel was right; it must have looked funny. He turned to see her smiling at him through the rain, her hair hanging in wet tendrils, her brown eyes glistening, and he couldn't help smiling back. 'I guess I must have looked pretty lame.'

'Lame? What is this word?'

'You know; stupid. Uncool.'

'Stupid, no. Funny, yes.'

'Yeah, well. Whatever.'

'You should smile more,' Isabel said. 'You look handsome when you smile.'

That took Ash by surprise. No one had ever called him that before. At least, not that he could remember. 'Maybe if I had something to smile about.' He turned his eyes to the river again, watching the white water froth around the edges and surge along the centre of its course. 'Everything's just so weird,' he said. 'Ever since I woke up, it's like . . . I dunno. It's like I'm not me any more. Except I *am* me.'

Isabel frowned. 'I don't understand.'

'Nor do I. Strange things are happening to me. I feel different.'

'Like hearing things?'

'Yeah. And seeing things I didn't notice before. Smelling things. And then, sometimes it's like everything is happening in slow motion and my reactions are quicker. I feel stronger too.'

'Like a superhero?'

'No.' He felt embarrassed at the suggestion. 'Not like that. More like . . .' He tried to think of a way to explain it. 'More like when you play a video game for the second time and it lets you keep all the upgrades.'

'You mean New Game Plus?'

'Yeah, except I'm *Ash* Plus. Like I've been wearing a see-through plastic suit all my life and now I've taken it off.'

'This is why you knew Thorn was there in the dark. You heard the boar, you smell things, you don't get tired in the jungle.'

'There's this too.' Ash held up his hand, glad to finally be talking about it. Glad that Isabel believed him. 'I cut myself with the knife before we left your house.'

'Right there?' Isabel pointed to the faint red line on his skin.

Ash nodded and unfastened his boot, pulling it off before removing his sock and unwinding the bandage. 'And these cuts are gone.' He grabbed his foot to look at the sole, and the rain washed away the dried blood, revealing unbroken skin beneath.

'That's not normal,' Isabel said.

'No.' Ash put his sock and boot back on. 'So what the hell is happening to me? Is it this island?'

Isabel shrugged. 'I have never seen anything like this before.'

'And all this stuff in my head. I thought it was going to drive me crazy.'

'It still feels like that?'

'I'm getting used to it.' Ash tried to put his feelings into words. 'It's like . . . like if you go somewhere new, you notice things, but after a while you stop noticing them unless you really look, or unless something changes. Well, when I notice, or really concentrate, I can smell all kinds of things, see things. I can even hear your heartbeat.'

'So what do I smell like?'

Ash remembered back to the first time he had seen Isabel. 'Sweet ginger, cinnamon, coconut. And a little sweaty.'

Isabel snorted. 'Well, it *is* hot here.'

'And . . .' Ash closed his eyes and focused on Isabel. 'And—' He opened his eyes and looked at her.

'What?'

Ash shook his head.

'*Kronos*,' Isabel said. 'It's inside me, isn't it? You can smell it. It wasn't just inside the lab, it was everywhere.'

Ash turned away.

'But you don't have it. It doesn't affect you, does it?'

He shook his head.

'I can feel it.' Her voice was quiet. 'I am getting sick.'

'No. Maybe you're just tired and—'

'But you can *smell* it.'

She was right. The scent of cooker gas was all around her, but now there was something else too: a sickening sweetness, like overripe fruit just on the turn, with a thread of rancid milk knotted through it. He knew at once that it was the smell of death – the stink of *Kronos* slowly destroying her body.

'I don't want to die,' she said.

'You won't.' Ash put a hand to the tag round his neck. What happened to Dad might have been his fault, but nothing like that was ever going to happen again. 'You're going to be fine. Cain and Pierce are out there and they have the cure. We'll find them. We'll find them and everyone will be fine. You, Mum, your dad. *Everyone.*'

But when Isabel looked at him, he saw the doubt in her eyes.

18 hrs and 43 mins until Shut-Down

One hundred metres wide, the river rushed through the forest, unstoppable and without mercy. Even in the shallows it moved at speed, but in the centre it was a raging monster, smashing against ragged rocks that rose from the spray like twisted teeth. It spewed foam and roared with energy that could snap bones as easily as matchsticks.

Ash's muddy boots ground the wet pebbles underfoot as he ventured closer to the edge. Clothes heavy with grime, he climbed onto a large black boulder to look into the seething water. The wind rushed around him, displaced by the ferocity of the water just a few metres away. He was mesmerized by the awesome power of what he was seeing. The wounds on his feet and hands might have healed faster than normal, but if he fell into that violent torrent he wouldn't have a chance; it would force him under and send him tumbling to his death. If he didn't drown, he would crack his head on one of those huge rocks and it would split his skull, just like it would split *any*one's.

'Do we really have to cross this?'

'Yes.' Isabel climbed up beside him. She looked like an explorer, with dirty streaks on her face, the pack and rifle slung over her back, standing in the softening rain.

Ash watched her, hoping that she could stay tough. Her heart was beating fast, but it sounded strong. She was hot, but not feverish, she smelt no more unwell than before, and—

'Stop it.'

He felt a flush of embarrassment. He hadn't meant to . . . what could he call it? Was there a word for using all your senses to find out how a person is feeling?

'It's like you're reading me. Don't.'

Read. That was it. He had been *reading* her.

'Yeah. Sorry. Um, is there some kind of bridge?' He glanced both ways along the river. To the left, it coursed round a bend, disappearing into the forest, but on the right there was a long, straight stretch before it vanished among the trees at the base of a large mountain.

'No bridge,' Isabel said. 'But there is a way to cross.' She pointed downriver towards the bend.

'I don't see anything.'

'Another five to ten minutes walking and you will.' She

climbed from the rock and shucked the rifle from her shoulder. She removed her rucksack and dropped it on the shingle before rotating her neck and stretching her muscles.

'You think the others got across?' Ash jumped down.

'I think they crossed much further upriver, before the rain. When the river was calmer, they could swim it.'

'What about the crate? How would they get that over?'

'Maybe it floats.'

Ash thought about the way the soldiers had kept hold of the wooden box when they had backed away from the crashing helicopter. It was important to them. 'What do you think's inside it? It had air holes. You think it might be some kind of animal?'

'We can ask them when we find them.' Isabel gave up trying to ease the tension in her aching muscles and shoul-dered the rucksack. She placed the rifle butt on the shingle and leant on the weapon for a moment. Her eyes were a little more bloodshot than before and every breath was now accompanied by a gentle rasping sound from deep in her chest. 'I don't feel so good, but I guess you know that. You have to listen to me,' she said. 'In case I can't go on.'

'What are you talking about?'

'I'm tired, Ash. Maybe too tired.'

'No. You're not getting out of this. You have to—'

'Just listen. I will try to keep going, but if something happens, you need to know where to go.'

'I'll carry you if I have to.'

Isabel smiled. 'We'll go to the crossing, and on the other

side we follow a path through the jungle to a pool. There is a place there to spend the night. Shelter. From there, we can walk along the ridge towards the bay. It's the same direction the others will have to go, but faster, so maybe we catch up with them or get to the boat first. Maybe we are already ahead of them.'

Ash remembered Mum's instructions. She had been clear. She wanted them to stop Pierce from leaving the island at all costs. She wanted *that* to be their priority. But Ash had other ideas. 'If we see them, we go after the cure,' he said.

'Of course. What else?'

'We're not going for the boat, like Mum wanted; we're going for the cure. That's our primary objective. The boat is secondary. It's optional.'

Ash knew about primary and secondary objectives from playing video games. Primary objectives delivered the main reward, secondary objectives delivered a bonus, and right now Ash wasn't interested in the bonus.

18 hrs and 28 mins until Shut-Down

Ash had been hoping for a bridge, but what he got was a rope and a small wooden cradle.

'Seriously?' He looked at the contraption that was swinging a few metres out over the river. 'We have to use *this*?'

The rope stretched from one side of the river to the other, looping back again and passing through a pulley at each side. The pulleys were secured to the trunks of stout trees on opposite banks, ten metres above the level of the water. Attached by cords to the top loop of the rope was what looked like a wooden pallet from a builder's yard – five planks laid side by side and fixed in place by thicker pieces of wood nailed to the bottom. The only thing that made it look any different from something that might be used to stack bricks was that someone had attached a small handrail to two opposing sides.

'Is it even safe?'

'Of course.' Isabel clambered up the bank to the tree where the rope was secured. She climbed up onto a rock, grabbed the rope and began hauling it hand over hand, bringing the cradle towards her. 'Come. Help me.'

Isabel was sick and weakening, but she showed no fear. Ash knew he should do the same, be strong for her, so he joined her on the rock and tried to grab the platform as it came nearer. At first it swung out of reach, but when it swung back he managed to snatch it and pull it close.

'Hold it while I get on,' Isabel said, but as soon as she jumped up and put any weight on the cradle, it started swaying about like crazy. 'Steady!' she shouted as she brought one knee up onto the wood.

The whole contraption was swinging back against Ash, threatening to bash him in the head and knock him off the boulder, but he struggled on and managed to bring the cradle under control so Isabel could climb up and shuffle over to the far side. When she was settled, she looked at Ash as if it had been the easiest thing in the world. 'Now you.' She patted the space beside her.

'Together? Will it take the weight?'

Isabel shook her head like she didn't understand.

'Are you sure we can both get on this together?' he said. 'Don't you think we're too heavy?'

'You and me are just kids. We are not so heavy.'

Ash studied the cables holding the cradle suspended beneath the rope, then looked at the speed of the water as it thundered past, swollen by the rain running off the mountain. But that wasn't the only thing that made him reach for the comfort of the tag round his neck. Here on the bank, the cradle was at head height, but over the centre of the river, it would be suspended ten metres above it. Ash wondered if he would rather face Thorn – or hang high above the raging river. 'You sure this is a good idea?'

'We'll be quicker together,' Isabel said. 'There's no other way to cross.'

Ash tore his eyes from the water and looked up to see her watching him.

'Is it the height?' she asked.

'Yeah. The height.'

'It is good there aren't any small dogs,' Isabel joked. But Ash didn't smile, so she frowned and became serious. 'The river will be like this for hours,' she said. 'There is no other way.'

'Right. Yeah.' He reached up to grab the lip of the platform. It dipped as soon as he put any weight on it, and began to swing and rotate – first one way, then the other. Ash used all his strength to keep from falling off as he kicked his feet in mid-air, dragging himself on board where there was just enough room for them to sit side by side, wedged between the handrails.

'It feels higher than it looked.' The swinging and twisting motion made his stomach queasy.

'Ready?' Isabel asked. She was sitting with the rifle in

front of her, the sling tucked firmly beneath her bottom to stop it from sliding away. The rucksack was still on her back.

Ash glanced up at the suspension cords and watched the way the line tightened and bowed under their weight. 'Not really.'

Isabel snorted through her nose, a kind of laugh, and patted Ash on the shoulder. 'We'll be OK. A few minutes and we'll be on the other side.'

'Right then.' He tried not to think about the height, tried not to look at anything but the rope. 'How do we make it work?'

'Easy.' Isabel was already holding the lower loop in both hands, and now she began hauling it towards her.

The cradle lurched, swung backwards and forwards, then inched out across the water.

'Help me pull,' she said, so Ash reached across her to grab the rope, and tugged as hard as he could.

The platform pitched forward with a jerk, the rifle slipping along the rough wood then pulling taut against the strap tucked under Isabel's bottom. Both Ash and Isabel slid closer to the edge of the platform, making them dig their heels into the cracks between the boards and scramble backwards. In turn, that upset the balance, making it tip in the other direction.

'Not so hard!' Isabel gripped the rope tight, trying to stop them from swinging. 'You want to make us fall?'

'Sorry.' Ash had his fists tight round the line, and his forearms burnt with the strain of trying to keep the platform steady. 'I guess I don't know my own strength any more.'

'Well, you need to learn. Don't pull so hard or we go in the water.' Isabel looked at him with a serious expression, before a smile cracked her lips, flashing those white teeth again. 'Your face, though. You looked funny.'

'Yeah,' he said. 'Hilarious.'

A few centimetres to his left and ten metres down, the fastest, most dangerous river Ash had ever seen was rushing through a deadly, rocky course.

Above him, the fixings groaned and creaked like they were about to give way.

Behind him, the most frightening man he had ever known was following, and ahead were the people who had shot down a helicopter and infected everyone in the BioSphere.

On top of all that, he had to find Pierce, get the cure for *Kronos*, recover Mum's notes and make it back to the Bio-Sphere in less than twenty hours. *And* save the world. So really, there was nothing funny about what was happening.

Nothing at all.

But despite everything, it was exhilarating. It was dangerous – *terrifying* – but the most important thing was that he was doing something. He wasn't cowering in a corner wondering what to do; he was out here, trying to stop Cain and Pierce. And Ash told himself that if Isabel could do this, then he could too. So he tried to ignore what was beneath him as they held onto the rope and waited for the platform to stop swinging. And when it had settled, they hauled on it once more and slipped further out over the raging water.

As they moved closer to the centre, the sound of the

water grew louder and louder so that it was thundering in his head. It was all he could hear as they pulled and pulled, dragging the platform slowly onwards, with the sun over their left shoulder drying their rain-soaked clothes.

It's all going too well, said the voice, but Ash shook it away. He and Isabel were going to do this. They were making good time and they would catch up with Cain and Pierce. Ash would not lose Mum like he had lost Dad.

When they were almost over the middle of the river, Ash summoned the courage to glance back and see how far they had come. 'Feels like we've been doing this for ages,' he shouted, 'but it doesn't look like we've come very far.'

Isabel shifted to look over her shoulder. 'A few more minutes and we'll be on the other side.'

A flurry of birds burst from the trees on the bank behind them, flitting out across the water and turning to fly down-river.

'What was that?' Isabel asked.

'Just birds.'

'No,' she said. 'Something made them fly up. You can see better than me – look in the trees where the birds came out.'

Ash shifted his attention from the distant birds and scanned the line of the jungle, seeing a wall of green and brown swaying in the breeze that followed the storm. There was the odd splash of red or yellow where flowers were growing, but other than that . . . 'I don't see any—'

Then he saw it. Close to the place where a branch forked from the trunk of a large, dark tree. He narrowed his eyes. 'Is that . . . ? My God, it's a face. Someone's watching us.'

'A *face*?'

'Thorn.' As soon as the word was on his lips, Ash knew it was true. Thorn was out there. He had caught up with them and he was watching them from the forest.

'But how?' Isabel said. 'We left no tracks. And why follow us and not Cain?'

'Makes no difference. We have to get moving.' Ash pulled harder on the rope, forgetting about the height and the raging river below. The platform tipped forward, but he didn't waste time trying to keep balanced. He tugged again, dragging them further along the rope, closer to the far bank.

Isabel steadied herself and grabbed the rope, trying to pull in time with him but finding it impossible to match his speed and strength.

'We'll cut it,' she panted. 'When we reach the other side. He can't follow then.'

'You sure there's no other way to cross?' Ash felt exposed and vulnerable, dangling over the river. If Thorn had a rifle, he could easily pick them off. Or maybe *he* would cut the rope and let the river take them.

'Not here,' Isabel said between breaths. 'Only way is to swim, but the current is too strong now.'

Ash continued to grab and pull. Isabel continued trying to keep up. The cradle swung backwards and forwards as they moved.

Progress was slow, but they were sliding over the centre of the current, passing the halfway point.

Grab and pull.

Ash glanced back to see if Thorn was still there, but it was difficult to tell. The cradle was swinging almost out of control, and he was only making it worse with his frantic attempts to reach the other side.

Grab and pull.

The fixings groaned once more and the cradle came to a sudden stop.

'¡Dios!' Isabel shouted, looking up and pulling hard again.

The cradle refused to budge, though, and instead tilted forward with a violent lurch. They both slipped down the damp wood, digging their boot heels into the slats, trying to find a decent grip.

'It's jammed,' Ash said, and his first thought was that it had something to do with Thorn, but when he looked back there was no one on the bank, and he could no longer see the face among the trees.

'Harder,' Isabel shouted, giving the rope another tug. Once again, the cradle lurched forwards and she leant back, digging her heels in to keep aboard.

'Stop!' Ash said. 'You're going to tip us over.'

'We must pull harder,' Isabel insisted. 'This happened before.'

'You sure?'

'Yes. Pull harder and it will come free.'

Ash tightened his grip on the rope. 'All right. On three?'

Isabel nodded. 'One. Two. *Three.*'

They leant back and pulled as hard as they could.

'We moved,' Ash said. 'I'm sure we moved.'

'Again. One more time.'

They secured their grip once more and Isabel counted off again.

'One. Two. *Three.*'

The rope remained stubborn for a second, then it released with a suddenness that made Ash and Isabel drop back with a jolt. The rope slid through their hands and the cradle moved forward.

'Yes!' Isabel looked at Ash with triumph. 'We—'

The cradle dropped a few centimetres.

Isabel's eyes widened and she stared at Ash for a second before they lifted their gaze to the rope from which the cradle was suspended. It had begun to sag under their weight.

'No . . .' Isabel said.

Then it snapped.

18 hrs and 14 mins until Shut-Down

The cradle dropped away, tipping to one side and spilling them out. Ten metres below the snapped line, it struck the water and whisked away in the current. A fraction of a second later, Ash hit the surface and went under in a rush of bubbles. He started tumbling as soon as the river had him. He saw sky, water, sky again. He caught glimpses of the bank, followed by nothing but bubbles. A flash of blue sky, a snatch of someone running out onto the pebbles.

Is that Thorn?

Water again.

The figure on the shore. A slender man, running along the bank.

Then nothing but water, filling his mouth. Rushing in his ears. Adding weight to his clothes. The might of it was all around him, rolling him over and over, scraping him along the stony bed. He was thrown up into the main current, then forced back down again, jarring against boulders like he was a toy.

Need to breathe.

He could do this.

With a surge of energy, Ash kicked out again and again until his feet came into contact with the riverbed. As soon as he felt it beneath him, he pushed away, shooting upwards, breaking the surface and taking a great gulp of air.

A few metres ahead, a black crag rose from the centre of the course, armed with brutal corners and sharp edges. It didn't matter that Ash was stronger and quicker than before – the rock would smash him to pieces just the same. At first the water clung to him, its frothing fingers refusing to let him go as it steered him towards the rock, but he fought hard to break free. As one part of the river released him, allowing another to take him, he skirted past the deadly rock, missing it by an arm's length, bringing him closer to the cradle that was buffeting just out of reach in the thick of the current.

The depths sucked at his legs, trying to drag him deeper. The surface pummelled him, threatening to push him down or break him against the rocks, but he had to get to that cradle. It was his only hope.

As soon as the wooden platform was within reach, Ash

boosted towards it, fingernails raking along the boards. Splinters needled his skin as the river wrestled to tear it from his grip. The river rushed in his face, sloshing into his mouth, trying to steal his breath, but he finally heaved himself aboard.

Ash clung to the ropes that were now wrapped around it, and pulled himself up, lifting his head to search the river.

'Isabel!' He could hardly hear his own voice over the sound of the water. 'Isabel!'

He watched the river, frantically looking for a sign. A flash of colour, a shape in the water.

There. Right in front of him. Something was waggling through one of the slats in the platform. Ash stared, trying to figure out what it was. Then, with a sickening sense of dread, it dawned on him. They were fingers.

'Isabel!'

She was caught in the ropes tangled around the cradle. She was trapped beneath him, underwater. Unable to breathe.

Letting go with one arm, Ash scrambled closer to the edge and reached under the cradle to feel Isabel lodged there. She reacted to his touch as he grasped whatever he could – shirt or trousers or hair, it didn't matter – and pulled hard.

She didn't budge.

'Come on!' he screamed as he tugged again. 'Come on!'

Isabel still didn't budge and Ash knew he couldn't waste time trying again; he had to get her some air. Thinking quickly, he moved back on the cradle and dropped into the water. He held tight and pushed down with all his strength, trying to tip the platform. Nothing happened, though; he was too small and light. He needed *more* weight, *more* strength, so he tucked his legs underneath the platform and pushed up with his feet while pulling down with his hands.

Finally, the heavy pallet began to tilt, the far end lifting up in the water until it was upright. Ash strained with effort, tipping the platform further and further until it flipped and toppled towards him. He had just enough time to grab hold of the ropes before it slammed down on top of him, forcing him deep into the water. When the rope tightened, he stopped with a jolt and was dragged along, clinging to the underside of the cradle.

Ash forged through the current, dragging himself hand-over-hand up the rope until he exploded from the surface of the water and grabbed for the slats on the upper side of the platform. Finding a secure purchase, he pulled himself aboard.

Isabel was right there, lashed to the cradle by the tangle of ropes, face down, with her head turned away from him. His first thought was that he was too late. Isabel was dead. She had drowned because he had been too slow to save her.

He clambered towards her and put his hand on her back, terrified that she was dead. He was filled with the sense that he hadn't done enough, that it was his fault, just like what happened to Dad had been his fault, but then Isabel groaned and lifted her head, coughing out muddy river water. She paused, bedraggled like a drowned rat, then turned to look at him.

'*Gracias,*' she whispered.

Ash closed his eyes and lowered his head onto the wood beside Isabel as all those horrible feelings washed away down the river. He *had* saved her. He really had.

He had saved Isabel just like he was going to save Mum.

'*Gracias,*' she said again.

'*De nada.*'

18 hrs and 08 mins until Shut-Down

The platform turned and bobbed as it washed down-river, but they had already survived the worst of it. By the time Ash flipped the pallet and brought Isabel above water, the main course of the river had widened further and the current had spread across its width. This gave it more space to accept the heavy rainwater pouring off the mountain.

'You all right?' Ash asked. Their faces were just centi-metres apart, their eyes locked together.

'Yes. Cut me loose.'

Unclipping the knife from his belt, Ash touched the razor-sharp blade to the ropes. 'Hold tight.'

It wasn't as easy as simply cutting in one place, so it took some effort to free her, but Isabel clung to the boards until Ash had sliced through the last piece and the ropes fell away into the water. He jammed the knife back into its sheath, then they took up position side by side on the pallet, with their legs trailing in the river, acting as rudders.

'Over there.' Isabel pointed to a place on the right where the bank eased into the water. It was flat and covered with pebbles, and if they could reach it, they would be able to escape the river's hold on them. 'We have to kick hard.'

So they kicked like maniacs, inching towards the edge of the main current and finally breaking free of it. From there it was much easier, and it wasn't long before they saw the pebbles beneath the stiller water.

'I can touch the bottom,' Ash shouted, and he slipped off the platform so he was standing waist deep.

Isabel did the same and they let go of the pallet, watching it spin in lazy turns as it drifted back towards the place where the river ran white. Eventually the current caught it once more and it whipped away.

Exhausted, they sat on the pebbles and stared at the river that had almost killed them. Isabel's skin was white and there was a trickle of blood from her nose. 'So I guess we *were* too heavy.'

'Yeah. I guess so.'

'But we survived. Maybe it will help with your fear of heights?'

'I think it's made it worse. And we lost everything.' His satchel was gone, the rifle, and Isabel's backpack too.

'We still have our knives,' Isabel said. 'We can survive.

And we were lucky. There is a waterfall that way.' She tipped her bruised chin to indicate downriver. 'We would have both been killed if you hadn't . . .' Her chin quivered like she was about to cry, and she wiped her hands across her face. 'You were very brave.'

'So were you.' Seeing her bloodshot eyes made Ash think about Mum, and for a moment he was back in the lab, reading the message she had typed on the tablet computer.

He glanced at Isabel's watch. 'Does it still work?'

Isabel turned her wrist and nodded. 'Shockproof. Waterproof.'

'How long have we got?'

'Eighteen hours.'

'We should get moving.' Ash pushed to his feet and held out a hand to help Isabel up.

'You're right.' She accepted the offer and pulled herself up beside him. 'We have only two hours before it gets dark.' She pointed into the forest. 'This way.'

'Thorn was there,' Ash said as they trudged deeper among the trees. 'When the rope snapped and we went into the water, I saw him on the bank. I think he was shouting something at me.'

'Shouting what?'

'I don't know.'

'Well, it doesn't matter now. He must be far behind us. The rope is gone and there's no other way to cross when the river is so fast. Things turned out good for us.'

'Except we almost died,' Ash said. 'And now we're soaking wet. Oh, *and* we've lost all our gear. It's my fault – I don't know my own strength any more. A few days ago, I couldn't even do ten push-ups but now . . . I don't know. I need to be more—'

'Careful.'

'Exactly.'

'No, I mean *be careful*.' Isabel stopped and pointed to the ground. 'Don't stand there.'

Ash glanced down to see a mass of ants marching from left to right across his path. They were big, at least five centimetres long. They had narrow bodies and huge heads with strong mandibles, and there were thousands of them, clambering over one another, moving in a wide, red-and-black column. When Ash focused, he could hear their movement as they passed across the forest floor – the scuttling of a million legs moving against one another, and the snipping of jaws as they tore through the insects in their path. The ants swarmed over everything, leaving nothing untouched, and their sound was like a heavy downpour of rain.

Ash pushed the noise away and watched as a mass of ants broke away from the line and came towards him. 'What are they doing?'

'Don't move,' Isabel whispered.

'They're coming for us.' Ash took a step back.

'Stay still,' Isabel hissed. 'They hunt by movement.'

'They *hunt*?' Ash froze and stared as the mass came towards them. Closer and closer until they were almost touching. He imagined them crawling up his legs and swarming over him, but he remained still as they moved closer. It was as if the ground was boiling in front of him, but then they stopped. As one, the insects came to a sudden halt, with their antennae feeling the air and their scissor-like mandibles opening and closing.

'Just stay still,' Isabel said in a near-whisper.

Ash remained frozen to the spot as the ants tasted the air for a few long seconds before turning and continuing back to meet their original path. Now, instead of a line, the ants were marching in a curve that came close to Ash and Isabel, then moved away from them.

'What's that all about?' Ash let out his breath but still didn't dare move. 'It's like they were checking us out.'

'Not us, I think. *You.* They know we are here, but they don't come to us because of you. Just like the boar stopped, and the insects don't bite you . . .' Isabel glanced at Ash.

'You think I'm some kind of freak?'

'Ash Plus?' Isabel raised her eyebrows. 'I don't know.'

'Great!' His voice was heavy with sarcasm.

'It doesn't matter what you are. You are my friend and you saved my life many times. In the BioSphere, Thorn would have killed us. The boar. The river. And now the giant soldier ants.' Isabel pointed to a mass of black writhing bodies at the base of a nearby tree. The ants were piling around each other, forming an enormous, seething ball. 'They make a nest out of themselves at night, then move on when the sun comes up.'

'Gross.'

'They're very dangerous,' she said. 'They eat everything in their way. Walking into an army of them would be like walking into a pool full of piranhas. I have heard of people leaving their villages because they have seen soldier ants coming, but here on *Isla Negra* they are the biggest I have ever seen.'

It didn't surprise Ash. *Everything* on Black Island was bigger, stronger and more dangerous than anywhere else.

'If you stand on them, they would cover you in seconds.'

'Would they eat a person?'

'If there are enough, they would eat anything.' Isabel tore her eyes from the mass of insects. 'Come. We must keep going.'

They took quiet, careful steps as they moved into the jungle, leaving the ants behind. Ash scanned up and down, afraid of what he was going to stand on as well as what might fall on him from above. He would have been happy if he never saw another insect in his life. Looking around like that, though, rather than just staring at Isabel's back, he realized something he hadn't noticed before. 'Are we on a path?'

'Yes. Papa and I have come this way, but we didn't make the path. I think it was here many years ago.'

'Made by who?'

'Papa said soldiers were here.'

'Soldiers? From where?'

'You will see.'

16 hrs and 18 mins until Shut-Down

When they finally reached the pool, it was like stepping into an oasis. The place was carpeted with flat, moss-draped rocks, as green as envy. Trees grew around them in a rough circle, as if it were sacred ground, the trunks leaning forward in prayer. Complicated root systems snaked around and over the rocks. The sweet smell of fresh water filled the cool air and the sound of a babbling stream chattered somewhere out of sight.

About twenty metres from the trees, the pool itself was so clear and still that if it wasn't for the fallen tree lying in its shallows, distorted slightly by the water, Ash might not have even realized it was there.

Isabel stopped and bent at the waist, putting her hands on her thighs. She stayed that way for a moment, catching her breath, then scanned the clearing. 'This is where we come. Papa and me. We walk here when he wants to get away from the BioSphere.'

'I can see why.' There was a sense of freshness there, as if the water gave up its coolness to the air. Ash tore his eyes from it and looked at Isabel, seeing the way she frowned and bit at her lower lip. He could tell she was thinking about her dad.

Isabel sniffed and reached back to unfasten her ponytail. She let the hairband roll over her wrist, and when she had gathered her hair together once more, she tied it back again, pulling it tight. 'It will be dark any moment,' she said. 'We should get inside.'

'Inside?'

Isabel pointed to the vegetation at the left side of the pool, but Ash saw nothing.

'And what do you mean, "It'll be dark any moment"?'

'It gets dark quickly.'

She wasn't joking. It took no more than a few minutes to pick their way across the rocks, but by the time they got to the place Isabel had pointed to, the sun was already dropping and much of the light had gone from the day.

'Animals sometimes come to the pool at night,' she said. 'It is better not to be outside.'

'What kind of animals?'

'I have seen boar prints here.'

A vision of that huge, ugly creature with tusks big enough

to rip a man in half, popped into Ash's head. 'Fantastic.' Ash reached down to put one hand on his knife as they came closer to the trees on the left side of the pool. He could now see that something was there – some kind of moss-covered structure hidden by the jumbled mess of trees and intertwined branches. 'What is this place?'

'From when the soldiers were here.' Isabel brushed away a hanging trail of vines to reveal a rusted metal door. She put her shoulder to it and pushed hard, the metal groaning as it swung open.

The musty smell that flooded out was a combination of concrete dust, decay and a thousand years' worth of stale air. There was something else too, something that clawed at the back of Ash's throat and burnt the inside of his nostrils like strong mustard.

They're waiting for you in there, whispered the voice. *Monsters in the dark. And they want to tell you a secret. Can you keep a secret?*

'Is it safe?' He chased the voice away. 'It looks . . . creepy.'

'It *is* creepy,' Isabel said, 'but it's fine.'

'And what's that smell?'

Isabel shrugged. 'Bats, I think.'

'And I'm guessing they're bigger than normal bats?'

'Maybe a little.'

'Do we have to go in there? Maybe we should just keep going?'

Isabel shook her head and looked back the way they had come. 'It is better to be inside. It will be cold at night, and dangerous.'

Ash remembered the boar, the outlandish ants, and wondered what animals Isabel hadn't told him about. He imagined monstrous crocodiles in the pool, and wild cats slinking through the trees.

'We need to rest and get dry,' Isabel said. 'It is very bad to be so wet in the jungle. We'll get sick and be no good for anything.' She looked at Ash for a second when she said the word 'sick', and Ash knew they were both thinking the same thing.

Isabel was *already* sick. And she was getting worse by the hour.

'We need a fire.' Isabel turned away and Ash followed her gaze, seeing that the pool was now shrouded in a grainy light. There was a faint mist seeping in from among the trees on the other side, washing around the shore. The sun was dropping quickly and it felt as if the forest was closing in around them.

As he watched, a chilling growl sounded through the jungle. It began as a low grumbling and grew louder until it was the sound of hell itself. It echoed from the rocks and spun around the pool, searing right through him.

'Howler monkeys,' Isabel said. 'The loudest sound in the jungle.'

'It's horrible.' The eerie noise pulsed in and out, as if some terrifying beast was crying out in pain. It was joined by other similar voices, all of them growling like devils until the air was thick with the sound and it was impossible even for Ash to distinguish one from another.

'We should go inside,' Isabel said. 'There is dry wood and

we can light a fire.'

'Good plan.' Suddenly, the idea of bats wasn't so bad. Ash cast his eyes around the trees and thought about Cain and Pierce out there somewhere. Thorn too. Isabel had said Thorn wouldn't be able to cross the river and follow them, but there was something inhuman about him. He had found Ash and Isabel in the darkness of the BioSphere, he had escaped the storeroom without any light, and he had followed them through the jungle even though they had left no trace.

'D'you know what time it is?'

'About six.' Isabel turned to him as if she knew what he was thinking. 'The sun will rise at about six, also.'

'That's twelve hours,' Ash said. 'We can't stay here that long.'

'We'll rest for a while and get dry.' Isabel put her hand on his shoulder. 'Please. We'll see what kind of moon it is. Maybe there will be enough light to travel at night. Maybe . . . maybe the animals will leave us alone because you are here, but we should rest a while at least.' She wasted no more time, using the last of the light to pick fruit from the trees that grew clustered around the concrete building.

'Why are there so many fruit trees here?' Ash asked. 'It's like someone planted them.'

'Not planted,' Isabel said. 'They grow here because people threw the seeds on the ground.' She reached up to tug a large yellow fruit from a tree with spreading fronds like a short palm. 'They were here a long time ago – seventy years, Papa said.'

'But why? What is this place?'

'It was a place for soldiers,' she said. 'We are close to Panama, where the canal is, so it was important in the war. And *Isla Negra* has many unusual plants and animals, so maybe they did experiments here.'

Out by the pool, a long creaking sound joined that of the howler monkeys.

'Frog,' Isabel said. 'Nothing to be afraid of.' As if in reply, the sound repeated, followed by another answering from further away.

'What about the monkeys?' Ash asked. 'Will they come here?'

'Maybe.' She shrugged. 'But they have never been dangerous.'

15 hrs and 57 mins until Shut-Down

The old war bunker was littered with rubble and the walls were crawling with moss.

'Be careful where you stand,' Isabel said.

Close to the door there was a large, tattered opening where the floor had collapsed into the darkness below. Metal reinforcement bars protruded from the edges like a witch's clawing fingers. Chunks of concrete clung to them in places. There was a similar hole in the ceiling, which would have let in light during the day.

They skirted round the hole and went deeper into the room. When they were a safe distance from it, Isabel put down the fruit and sank to the floor.

'How do you feel?' Ash didn't really need to ask, and he

didn't need to use his heightened senses to know that she was exhausted. For the first time since she had mentioned it by the river, Ash was beginning to consider that he might have to continue alone.

'We need to make a fire,' she said. 'But I don't think I can get my hands to work. I'm cold. Is it cold in here?'

'Yeah. It's cold.' Ash couldn't feel it, though. He hadn't been hot in the jungle and he wasn't cold now. 'You want me to try getting a fire going? You got matches or something?'

Isabel frowned. 'I had waterproof matches in my pack.'

'Oh.' Ash pictured all their gear being washed away down the river. 'Nothing else?'

'There is a fire steel on the sheath of your knife. You know how to use it?'

'I think so.' Dad had showed him a few different ways to make a fire without matches, so Ash pulled his knife from its sheath, grabbed a thin, dry stick from the woodpile and began whittling. He stopped every now and then to scoop the shavings together, and when there were enough he arranged a wigwam of sticks around it.

After that, he took out the fire steel and scraped the back of his knife along it. His first attempt was useless, so he repeated the action until he was showering the tinder with sparks. The ends of some pieces began to glow and small tendrils of smoke rose from them.

'That's it.' He cupped his hands around the wigwam, blowing gently until the flames grew, then sat back and fed the fire with more wood.

The orange, flickering light revealed a room about half the size of a school gym. In the far corner, a rotten table with only three legs was pushed up against the wall, leaning at an awkward angle. Underneath it was a pile of empty, rusted tins, a ragged mound of papers, a beaten-up typewriter and a rotten boot with the sole peeling away from the leather. There was a dirty tarpaulin there too, twisted and wrinkled like a decayed corpse. On the adjacent wall stood a wonky row of corroded filing cabinets, while one or two others lay on their sides like dead monsters. Thrown on top of them was a cage much like the kind a dog owner might have for their pet.

The walls were just bare concrete, but the one to the left of the entrance was painted with a faded black eagle with its wings spread wide.

Ash studied the eagle, with the growing sensation that he had seen it before. This exact one. Right here, on this wall.

You've been here before, said the voice. *But that's our little secret.*

No, that wasn't possible. He must have seen it in a picture. Maybe in a book. He went over to the table and touched the toe of his boot to the papers, trying to spark a memory.

'Papa said we have to leave everything as we find it. There might be something important here about the island.'

'What's through there?' Ash pointed to the door opposite the entrance.

'Other rooms. And some stairs going below. Papa said not to go. It's too dangerous.'

Ash nodded, but he wanted to know what was down there. He had such a strong sensation that he'd been here before, and he wanted to prove himself wrong. He went over to the fire to pull out a burning stick and then crept towards the edge of the hole.

'Be careful.' Isabel didn't need to tell him, though. As soon as he saw that gaping, bottomless pit, Ash had to stop himself from thinking about falling in. His stomach lurched the same way it had done when the rope snapped on the river crossing.

Dust cascaded from the broken edges as he inched closer; there was a soft sound down there, the shuffle of leathery wings. The light from the burning stick wasn't strong enough to reach the bottom, but daring to peer closer, Ash could see the light reflected in something below.

'There's water down there.' He let go of the burning stick and watched it fall for a couple of seconds before it hit a pile of rubble on the floor about seven metres below. It erupted in an explosion of sparks, causing a flurry of clicking and chattering that made him step back in alarm. When the sound died down and he risked another look, the stick had settled into a slowly fading burn and he could see that the room beneath was more or less the same size as the one they were in. Black, stinking water shimmered from wall to wall like an oil slick, and there was an island of rubble in the centre, where the floor above had caved in. Four or five rusted barrels lay part-submerged, and one wall was stacked high with cages. Others were lying in the rancid water. Ash could also make out a large table and a couple of benches, various bottles and jars, and more papers.

'Wouldn't want to fall down there,' he said. 'What is all that stuff?'

'Papa thinks it was used for experiments a long time ago. He said some of the papers look like research, but he didn't know what. The cages must have been for animals. Better to keep away, I think.' Warmed by the flames, Isabel was starting to sound better. She removed her boots and socks and placed them near the fire to dry, then lifted her T-shirt away from her body, wafting it in the heat. 'You did a good job with the fire,' she said. 'I'm sorry I—'

'Forget it.' Ash came back and sat beside her. He untied his laces and removed his boots. 'It's weird. I feel like I've seen this place before. It's like *déjà vu*. Do you know that word?'

'Yes,' she said. 'Maybe you have seen a photo.'

'Yeah, maybe.'

Isabel watched him across the fire, eyes sparkling. 'You hungry?'

'Starving.'

'We could catch some frogs and insects. Cook them on the fire. Very tasty.'

'Maybe I'm not that hungry, after all.'

Isabel snorted. 'Or we have these.' She picked up one of the large yellow fruits and cut it in half lengthways. She did the same thing again, separating it into four long pieces, then scraped away the black seeds before passing one to

Ash. 'Papaya,' she said, taking a large bite. 'Much better than frog.'

Ash sniffed the fruit, thinking it smelt like the Best Thing *Ever*, then nibbled the edge. The flavour exploded in his mouth like fireworks. Mum was always telling him to eat more fruit, that it was good for him, but if he had known it could taste like this he would have eaten *much* more of it. His fingers were sticky and the juice ran from the corners of his mouth as he wolfed down the soft, delicious flesh and put the rind to one side.

Isabel grinned and passed him another. 'Good, hmm? But we can go look for frogs if you don't like it.'

Ash shook his head and bit into his second piece. 'No way.' He began to settle for the first time since waking up in the white room. The glow of the fire and the crackling of the burning sticks was soothing, and the fresh woodsmoke hid the unpleasant smells of the building as it rose to escape through the hole in the ceiling. He thought about everything they'd been through and how good Isabel was in the jungle. 'You learn all that stuff from your dad? About the animals and fruits?' he asked.

Isabel nodded and put her second piece of rind beside the other. She sat back and crossed her legs, staring into the base of the fire. 'In San Jose – where we lived before Papa took this job – we sometimes travelled out to the forest at the weekend, and sometimes for longer. Papa grew up with it and wants me to know the forest too.' A distant smile crossed her lips. 'Mama loved the forest, but . . .' She stared into the fire, her eyes filling with tears. 'The smoke,' she lied.

'It always itches.'

'Did something happen to your mum?' Ash asked.

'She was very ill with malaria. It was a long time ago, but I miss her every day. Today I miss her a lot.' She wiped her eyes.

Ash watched her through the flames. 'My dad died.' His voice sounded like it belonged to someone else. 'Last week.' He reached out to take a stick from the pile, poking it at the base of the fire, making the glowing embers sparkle. 'It was all my fault.'

Isabel just sat there not saying anything. She wiped one hand across her eyes and waited for him to go on.

Ash shoved the stick right into the hottest part of the fire and held it there, wishing it were as easy to burn away the awful empty ache in his heart. 'Dad took the dog out for a walk and . . .' He tried not to think about the terrible sound Mum had made when the police came to the house. 'Dad was hit by a car.' He let go of the stick and looked up at Isabel. 'The car just drove away. The police still don't know who did it.'

Ash hadn't been there when it happened, but he had seen it over and over again, a million times in his head.

'But why do you say it was your fault?' Isabel asked.

'*I* was supposed to take the dog for a walk. It should have been me. He was *my* dog.'

'But that doesn't make it your fault. Your mama doesn't blame you.'

'Maybe not, but I do. *I* blame myself because I made such a fuss about going out that night. It was raining and cold and I didn't want to go, but Dad was so calm and just picked up his coat. The last thing I remember of him is the dog dragging him along the path and . . .'

His voice trailed off. It was the most he had said about it to anyone since it had happened. It felt good to get it out, like removing a splinter that was stuck deep in his skin. And Isabel didn't try to comfort him or say the right thing, like people usually did. She just sat there and listened.

'If I had gone out instead, then maybe it wouldn't have happened. Or maybe it would have been me that got hit.' Ash put his hand to the identity tag hanging on the leather cord around his neck. He turned the metal disc in his fingers. 'This was Dad's,' he said. 'One of his dog tags from the army. There's always two. He kept one and gave me the other. He wore it all the time and said I should too. He was wearing it when they—' He didn't want to remember, but there it was: the funeral, everyone in black, the coffin, Dad lying inside it with the other tag around his neck.

Isabel leant closer to see the shiny metal disc with the black plastic 'silencer' fitted around it. She read the name McCarthy, and saw a series of letters and numbers she didn't understand.

'It gives you courage,' she said.

'Yeah. Dad was so tough, and I think he wanted me to be like that too, but I never was. I'm scared of heights, the dark, spiders, just about everything. I don't know why; I just am. I always feel like such a wimp, and it doesn't help that most people in my year at school are bigger than me. He told me that when I was scared I should hold it and say the words,

"I am Ash McCarthy. I am strong. I can do this." That probably sounds lame, doesn't it?'

'No.' Isabel shook her head. 'It sounds strong. And look what we have done today; look how tough you have been. I think your papa would be proud of you.'

8 hrs and 36 mins until Shut-Down

Time. Time. Time. Everything was about how little of it was left.

The hard concrete floor was cruel to his lean frame. Within minutes of lying down, Ash's hips and shoulders had been aching. And there had been that creepy howl and moan of the monkeys outside. He had tried to ignore it, sometimes listening to the erratic rise and fall of Isabel's breathing, but he had been scared by the way her heart raced and fluttered.

Now he watched the flames flickering and dancing in the dark and realized that, despite his discomfort, he must have fallen asleep. He had that groggy, just-woken-up feeling and the fire had dried the air in the bunker, so his throat felt parched and sore.

You've got it too, the voice sniggered. *Kronos is inside you. It's in your blood. But that has to be our little secret. You can't tell anyone.*

He sat up with a start. 'What time is it?'

Isabel stirred from sleep and rubbed her face with both hands. It took her a moment to focus on her watch. 'Two,' she mumbled. 'In the morning . . . *¡Madre de Dios!*'

They had been asleep for hours. How could they have wasted so much time? How far ahead of them would Cain and Pierce now be?

'Look, we need to get out of here,' Ash said. 'We should check if there's enough light from the moon to keep going. And we need water. Can we drink from the pool?'

'No.' Isabel sat up and looked across at the rickety table and the rubbish lying beneath it. 'But we can collect water in one of those tins. Boil it over the fire to make it safe to drink.'

With a renewed sense of urgency, they rummaged in the pile of tins, searching for one without holes rusted in it. Seeing a good one at the bottom of the pile, Isabel tugged it out, dislodging the others so they fell and clattered around them. As they collapsed, a dark shape scurried out from the tangle and scuttled across the shadows on the twisted tarpaulin.

'Get away!' Isabel grabbed Ash by the arm so hard that he fell backwards.

'Ow, what're you doing?' He glared at her but she wasn't looking at him; she was staring at something to the right of the collapsed mound of tins. A dark shape sitting on the tarpaulin, swaying from side to side.

'Stay still.' Isabel shuffled to the fire and took out a burning stick before bringing it closer to the table. She held it at arm's length, illuminating a fat spider with a dark brown body, about twice the size of Ash's fist. Its legs spanned wider than an adult's hand at full stretch, and it was crouched back on four of those legs, with the front four held up in preparation to launch itself at Isabel. Its large fangs were shining in the firelight.

'Wandering spider,' Isabel said. 'Very dangerous. Very aggressive. On *Isla Negra* they are even—'

'– more aggressive than normal? And bigger?'

Isabel nodded and the spider turned towards her. She gently waved the burning stick to keep its attention. 'It could kill *both* of us.'

'Fantastic.' Ash looked about, searching for signs of other similar creatures. 'Perfect.'

'They are lonely spiders,' Isabel said.

'I'm not surprised.'

'I mean, there won't be others. Just this one.' She didn't take her eyes off the spider. 'But they can move fast.'

'As if I'm not creeped out enough already! Now it's *fast*? How do we get rid of it?'

'Maybe we can trap it. Pass me one of those tins,' Isabel said. 'A big one.'

'What? No way. It's too close to the spider.'

'Just do it!'

Ash crept across the floor while Isabel was distracting

the spider, and used a long stick to drag one of the tins towards him. The spider twitched and lifted its legs higher so that its fangs were aimed right at Isabel.

'Quick!' Isabel hissed. 'It's going to—'

The spider struck forward, fast as a bullet, but Ash reacted even faster. Faster than he thought possible.

Like before, when the glass ceiling collapsed in the BioSphere, Ash saw everything happening around him in slow motion. He saw the spider scuttle forwards. He saw its legs bend and straighten. He saw its coal-black fangs, curved and ready to sink into Isabel's skin.

In one quick movement, he snatched up the tin and scooped it through the air in front of Isabel. He caught the creature mid-jump, feeling the solid weight of its body hit the metal, then slammed the tin down onto the concrete floor, trapping it inside.

Then – *pop* – the world returned to normal.

'*¡Dios!*' Isabel jumped back, waving her hands in front of her to fend off the spider. It took her a fraction of a second to realize that it hadn't reached her, and as soon as she did she turned to look at Ash, then at the tin he was holding firm against the ground.

'*Madre de Dios,*' she whispered. 'That was so *fast!*'

Ash swallowed hard and nodded. His hands were shaking and the tin was rattling on the concrete floor. Inside, the spider was scuttling about, searching for an escape.

He remembered that Isabel had told him they tried not to harm anything on the island, but Ash wasn't taking any chances with the spider. He put his foot on the tin and stood up, applying as much pressure as he could. For a moment the tin remained intact, then it crumpled under his boot, crushing the monster inside. Brown goo oozed out from beneath and Ash stomped on the tin to flatten it completely, then kicked it into the fire.

When he looked up, Isabel was staring at him open-mouthed.

Ash shivered. 'I hate spiders.' He went to the door and pulled it open, needing to feel fresh air on his face. It squealed on rusty hinges, and the forest fell silent. 'In fact, I don't think I like *anything* in the jungle very much. It's just full of things to be scared of.'

'It's beautiful.' Isabel came to stand beside him.

'How can you say that? It's terrifying.'

'So are tigers, but they are still beautiful, aren't they?'

'I suppose.' Ash put his head back and let the breeze waft across his face. 'Is there enough light for us to keep going?' He looked up at the half-moon through the gap in the trees. It was surrounded by a billion stars. A *billion* billion. 'We can see in this light, can't we? At least, I can.'

'Look at the fireflies.' Isabel raised a hand and pointed over to the trees they had come through earlier that evening. Beyond the pool, dozens of tiny yellow lights flashed among the branches, flitting in a haphazard pattern.

'Sometimes, if the lights look red, people say it's the *cadejo*. He's an evil big black dog with red eyes who attacks travellers.'

'I don't think I want to know about that right now.'

Isabel laughed. 'It is only a story. And there is a white one too. A good one. Maybe we could hope for him to come.'

The fireflies formed a cloud in the trees, flickering together and beginning to drift towards Ash and Isabel.

'What are they doing?' Ash whispered, but Isabel could only shake her head as the glittering cloud approached, shrouding them in a constellation of sparkling stars.

For once, Ash was not afraid. He somehow knew the insects would not touch him. He heard the beat of their tiny wings and felt the faintest breeze on his cheeks.

'This is amazing,' Isabel said. 'I've never seen anything like this.'

Ash couldn't stop himself from smiling. He closed his eyes, putting his head back, and felt as if he were floating in space. Even with his eyes closed, he could see the fireflies flickering on the inside of his eyelids. When he opened them, though, he saw something else.

Something was watching them.

High in the branches of the closest tree, a howler monkey sat on its haunches, tail curled round the branch. It was at least Ash's height, with thick, muscular shoulders and a powerful back covered by glossy black hair with a faint grey stripe running the length of it. Its mouth was set in a tight expression, and it was staring directly at him.

'Look.' The familiar feeling of fear began to creep back.

Isabel glanced up and saw the monkey, but its eyes hardly even flickered to acknowledge her movement. Just like the monkeys in the lab, it was only interested in Ash.

'There are others,' Isabel said.

But Ash didn't need her to tell him. As he watched

through the cloud of shimmering fireflies, he spotted more monkeys sitting in the branches of the surrounding trees, perched like gargoyles on a church roof, all of them staring at Ash.

'What do they want?' he said. 'Why are they looking at me?'

Isabel shook her head. 'Maybe they are curious?' she guessed. 'Like the insects and the boar. Even the spider did not attack you. I think the way you are – they know you are different. They sense it.'

'What do you want?' Ash raised his voice to the nearest monkey.

The animal flinched as if it were about to dart away, but stopped with its head half turned towards the forest beyond the pool, eyes still fixed on Ash. Its body tensed, and its lips came forward to make an 'O' shape. It grunted, low and deep, then opened its mouth to bare its teeth. When Ash saw those sharp incisors jutting from its upper and lower jaws like daggers, he imagined them ripping into his flesh. He had always thought monkeys looked cute, but not these ones. These looked like vicious killers.

He took a step back, thinking it might be time to take cover in the bunker, but something else caught his eye. A bright flash, deeper in the forest. The light flickered again, but it wasn't the tiny yellow glow from a firefly. This was white and lasted much longer before it disappeared from view. It was accompanied by the sound of boots on the ground, and the heavy beat of breathing.

'Thorn is coming.'

'What?' Isabel didn't dare look away from the howlers. 'How could he find us? In the dark? How did he cross the river?'

'I don't know, but he's here.'

In the tree, the howler leant forward, put out its lips and grumbled. It was an unsettling sound – long and deep and croaking – and within a second or two, another monkey had joined it, then another and another, their pitch and tone changing. In just a few short moments, the night was filled with the whoops and grunts and barks of more howlers than Ash could count.

'I think they're warning us,' he said. 'Get back inside and close the door so Thorn doesn't see the fire.'

They backed into the room, watching the light flickering in the trees, heading in their direction. As soon as they were inside, they pushed the door shut.

'What do we do?' Isabel sounded scared.

Ash glanced around the room, then back at the door. 'I think I've got an idea.'

08 hrs and 01 mins until Shut-Down

When they were finished, Ash nodded and stepped away from the dampened fire. 'We're ready. You get back, I'll open the door.'

Creeping forward, he grabbed the handle, took a deep breath and yanked it wide. Like before, it screeched on its rusted hinges, but it was almost inaudible because the howlers grew more agitated, filling the night with their demonic grunting and growling.

'He's coming.' Ash hurried back to join Isabel in the darkest shadows of the bunker.

They huddled together, squeezed as far into the corner as possible. Earlier, Ash might have been worried about spiders crawling over him, but right *now*, the only thing he was scared of was Thorn. Right *now*, the only things he could think about were the broken bodies in the BioSphere and the man without expression.

(*He'll gut us both.*)

Between them and the door, the fire was little more than a gentle glow, so the room was almost in darkness, but there was enough light to attract Thorn's attention.

Outside, the monkeys raged as the light moved in the forest, flickering when Thorn passed behind the trees. Ash could have sworn he was following the exact route he and Isabel had taken, as if he were some kind of sniffer dog. Again, Ash had the fleeting thought that Thorn might be like he was. Thorn Plus.

'Maybe . . .' Isabel's dry tongue clicked. 'Maybe we should have hidden in the forest.'

'This'll work,' Ash said.

It won't, said the voice. *Thorn is going to take your knife and cut you down the middle.*

Ash touched the identity tag for reassurance, then looked down at the survival knife in his fist and gripped it tighter.

'He's there.' Isabel's whisper sent a shiver down his spine and Ash looked up to see the white light come to the edge of the trees. It stopped and scanned left to right, before shining towards the bunker.

They crouched together, knives held out in front of them, and watched as Thorn came right out into the clearing and angled his light towards the canopy, illuminating a frenzy of activity in the trees. The monkeys leant out from their perches, baring their teeth, grunting and howling. Thorn turned on the spot, surrounded by the baying animals, then flicked off his torch so he was nothing more than a dark shape. Then, like a ghost floating over the rocks, he moved quickly towards the bunker.

Isabel's breathing was loud. Ash could feel her fear as much as he felt his own. He could smell the acrid burnt plastic, mingled with the over-ripe sweetness of *Kronos* flowing through her veins, spreading its death.

But as Thorn approached, Ash could sense that the killer was unnerved too. The monkeys had scared him, and the way he moved wasn't like in the BioSphere. He wasn't as calm now. His heart was beating faster, his steps were less confident, and when he reached the bunker he came straight inside and pulled the door shut behind him.

The instant it closed, the howling stopped as if someone had pressed a button. Every monkey fell silent at once.

'Ash?' Thorn's voice was like a cold hand around Ash's throat. 'Isabel? Are you in here?' He stepped further inside and switched on his torch, shining it from wall to wall, finally coming to rest when it was pointing right into the far corner. 'Ash.'

Holding the knife at arm's length, Ash got to his feet and puffed out his chest. He spoke in a low, strong voice. 'Leave us alone.'

Thorn took another step into the room. 'You've given me quite the runaround.'

'Leave us alone.'

'I'm here to help. I tried to tell you before but you threw a crowbar at me. Good shot, by the way.'

'Help us?' Ash tried to read him – to listen to Thorn's breathing, to hear his heartbeat and sense if he was lying, but there was too much to think about. Too much to confuse him. 'No, you're here to *kill* us.'

Thorn took a step closer and pointed the torch at the wall, holding out his other hand. 'Kill you? No, Ash, you don't understand.' He took another step forward. 'I really am here to help you. Both of you. You have to list—'

Thorn's next step came down on the old tarpaulin they had dragged from beneath the table and draped over the hole in the floor. Before Thorn could finish his sentence, the thick material disappeared beneath him, and he fell forward. The torch flew out of his hands, clattering on the concrete, and he reached out, trying to grip the side of the hole. It was too wide for him, though, and he disappeared in the blink of an eye, vanishing into the darkness below.

There was a thump, followed by a sudden flurry of move-ment as a colony of large bats, disturbed by Thorn's fall, spiralled up in turmoil. They poured out from the room below, circling and chattering around the bunker, then made for the hole in the ceiling and vanished into the night.

When they were gone, an eerie silence fell over the room.

'It worked,' Isabel said. 'We got him.'

07 hrs and 49 mins until Shut-Down

Thorn's torch lay on the floor to one side of the gaping hole, the beam shining out in a cone that lit up the moss-patched wall beside the entrance.

Ash snatched it up and sidled to the edge of the hole. When he shone the light into the darkness, all he could see was Thorn's canvas survival pack hanging from an exposed reinforcement bar, then he saw the stinking black water and the wall lined with rusted cages, splattered with bat mess.

Isabel came to his side and spoke in an urgent whisper. 'Can you hear anything? You hear so good, I thought maybe you could use your . . . whatever it is. *Read* him.'

Seeing her expectant expression, Ash nodded and took a deep breath. 'I'll try.' He touched the tag round his neck and concentrated, pushing his fear deep inside.

There were so many sounds. The breeze whispering through the hole in the roof, the flicker of bats' wings outside, the lap of water in the room below, and—

'I hear him.' Ash looked at Isabel. 'It's quiet, but I can hear him breathing. He's alive . . . sounds hurt.'

'OK,' Isabel said. 'Let's see.' She held her knife in front of her, and together they moved closer to the edge of the hole to get a proper look.

Thorn was lying on his back on the pile of rubble in the centre of the room. The tarpaulin was tangled around him. His eyes were closed, but when Ash shone the torchlight on his face they eased open.

'Ash?' His voice was strained. 'You have to listen to me. I really am here to help.' He grunted in pain. 'I work for MI6. My job is to protect the world from threats like *Kronos*. We've been watching your mother for weeks . . . monitoring her work since we heard what she was doing. The people I work for think the virus she created is too dangerous.'

For a second, Ash was too shocked to say anything. 'She made the *cure*,' he blurted. 'Not the virus.'

'She made *Kronos* too, Ash.'

'No way. Why would she make something like that? Why would—'

'Because she works for BioMesa. And making pharmaceuticals is only a part of what they do. They research and create biological weapons.' Thorn stopped for breath, his chest wheezing. '*Kronos* is a weapon. In the wrong hands . . . it could kill everyone on the planet . . . in a matter of months.' He tried to sit up again, but the pain was too much for him. His eyes rolled up and he slumped back, taking quick shallow breaths.

Ash looked at Isabel. Everything had been flipped upside down. If Thorn was telling the truth, then it meant Mum wasn't some amazing scientist trying to save the world; she had, in fact, created a virus that could wipe it out.

Millions will die.

Below, Thorn let out a cry of pain and pushed himself up. He pulled the tarpaulin away from his lower body, revealing that the material of his trousers was torn down the right leg, and a sharp piece of shinbone had broken through his skin.

He looked up at Ash and Isabel. 'You'll have to stop Pierce and Cain on your own.'

'What?' Ash glanced at Isabel, seeing that she was just as confused, then looked down at Thorn. 'What are you talking about? You're *helping* them. You injected me. You killed all those—'

'No, I came here to stop them. My job was . . .' He sighed and rubbed his hand over his face. 'I need water. Please, I'll tell you everything. About the virus, about your mum. I have clean water. In my bag.' Thorn's words were quiet and strained. 'Painkillers too. Give them to me and I'll tell you what I know.'

Ash moved the torch beam around the edge of the hole to illuminate the canvas pack hanging from the reinforcement bar.

'We should leave him,' Isabel said. 'Go after Pierce and get the cure.'

'You heard what he said. I have to know about my mum. I mean—'

'And *I* have to have the cure,' Isabel snapped at him. 'My papa and your mama need it. *I* need it. We are going to die.'

'I can help with that,' Thorn said. 'I have the cure. It's right there in my pack.'

07 hrs and 33 mins until Shut-Down

Without hesitation, Ash reached down to grab the pack. He dragged it away from the place where it was snagged, and opened it as quickly as he could. He pulled out a syringe gun, shining like polished silver, and held it up to the light. It was the same as the ones they had seen in the lab.

'That's your cure,' Thorn said. '*Zeus.* Everyone on Cain's team was injected, but I kept a dose. Just in case.'

Ash looked at the syringe gun in his hand.

'Just put it against your arm and pull the trigger,' Thorn said. 'It's simple. I'm just sorry I only have one. You will have to decide which of you is going to have it.'

Isabel opened her mouth to say something, but Ash

shuffled forward on his knees and pressed the barrel of the gun against her upper arm. He squeezed the trigger and the needle came forward, releasing what he hoped was *Zeus* into Isabel's system.

'There.' Ash tossed the syringe away. 'It's done.'

'Very noble,' Thorn said. 'Now for my water and painkillers.'

Ash took a metal canister from a pocket on the side of the pack and dropped it down into the hole. Thorn groaned when it landed on his stomach, and grabbed it before it could roll away.

'Painkillers,' he said.

'As soon as you tell me about my mum.'

'There's a plastic box. Take it out. Let me see them.'

With an impatient sigh, Ash dug into the pack and found a white plastic box, with a red cross printed on the front. He popped it open and saw three narrow packets with a covering of foil, similar to a strip of tablets. Taking them out, he held them up for Thorn to see. 'Tell me everything you know and you can have them.'

Thorn took a sip of water and wiped his mouth. '*Isla Negra* is unique,' he said. 'There's nowhere else like it on earth. At least, not that anyone knows about. During the war, it was important because it's so close to the Panama Canal, but there was also a small research facility here.'

'You mean, like Nazi experiments?' Ash asked.

'No.' Thorn shook his head in a slow and weak movement. 'Most papers were destroyed, but scraps and fragments were found in different languages – German,

French, Japanese, English. Whatever they did, whatever *happened* here, it changed the island. It could have been a virus or bacteria that leaked and altered the nature of the microorganisms, maybe the re-introduction of animals used for experimentation . . . no one's sure of anything except that something changed this island. For many years it was left to . . . evolve. The buildings crumbled, but the forest and the animals changed. They *thrived*.'

'Which is why everything here is so weird,' Ash said. 'Why the animals are bigger. I get it, but what's that got to do with my mum?'

'When BioMesa came here, they noticed that the biggest changes occurred in one animal in particular. The monkeys.'

'The howlers.' Immediately Ash remembered the way they had watched him from the glass cages in the lab – how they had stared at him from the treetops. A shivering uneasiness tingled in his scalp. 'What kind of changes?'

'They were strong, intelligent, resistant to disease, able to adapt to almost anything. That's where your mother and Pierce became involved. They worked together on—'

'Mum *worked* with Pierce?'

'Mm-hm. A research black site – a secret facility – was established on the island. Your mother and Pierce came here more than ten years ago to investigate what was happening, and they became interested in the monkeys. Pierce thought he'd identified some kind of . . . mutation in their blood. Something that made them different; something that could be used to enhance human performance.'

Thorn paused and grimaced in pain.

Ash waggled the painkillers. 'Keep talking.'

'Pierce wanted to test his mutagen on humans, but the days when that was allowed were long gone, so he tested it on himself. It was a failure. Nothing worked. After that, all I know is that something happened between Pierce and your mother. Pierce's research was closed down, he was dismissed from the company and your mother left the island to continue working at BioMesa in England. That's where she isolated *Kronos* from blood taken from the howler monkeys living here. Swimming in their blood right alongside it was the antiviral, *Zeus.*'

'But that can't—'

'I know you don't want to believe it, Ash, but it's true. Your mother weaponized *Kronos*. She made it airborne – that means you can catch it the same way you catch a common cold.' Thorn winced as pain burnt through his leg. 'She was appalled, though, at what she had achieved. At how uncontrollable *Kronos* is. You have to believe that, Ash. All her energies were then focused on *Zeus*, on the cure.'

Ash thought back to the storage room in the BioSphere, to all that HEX13 nestled in the locker. What had Isabel said when he asked if they made guns there?

(*Not guns. Other kinds of weapons, I think.*)

'Pierce wasn't working for BioMesa any more but somehow he found out how far your mother had progressed with her research,' Thorn said. 'He demanded that his part in the discoveries should be acknowledged. He wanted the details of how to isolate the virus. He wanted *Kronos*, but your mother refused to give it to him – she feared he might sell it as a weapon, sell to the highest bidder. She believes it's too dangerous, too unresearched. It begins like flu, but develops fast, spreading through the internal organs in hours, making them bleed, like the Ebola virus. And once *Kronos* has done its worst, even *Zeus* can't save you.'

'Shut-Down,' Ash whispered.

'Your mother destroyed her research. Everything to do with *Kronos* was wiped from existence, and that made Pierce mad. He hired Cain's team to help him – to force your mother to give him what he wanted. We were to bring her here to reproduce her work from memory. A private jet to San Jose in Costa Rica, a helicopter to *Isla Negra* and here we are – the only place on the planet where Pierce could force your mother to recreate her work. He needed a lab and he needed those monkeys. This is the *only* place where the right blood can be found. And if she didn't do as he asked, you would be killed. We had intelligence to that effect, so I infiltrated the team back in England. My job was to stop them.'

In a daze, Ash stared down at Thorn. 'That's why they kept me asleep,' he said. 'So I was ready to be killed.'

'No one knows why you didn't wake up. But Pierce didn't care. He had you where he needed you, and when your mother's work on *Kronos* and *Zeus* was completed, Pierce planned to release the virus within the dome and lock down the BioSphere. Everyone was supposed to die in there, while we escaped with your mother's notes. With those, and just one monkey, Pierce would have everything he needed to make as much *Kronos* as he wants. But things went wrong when your mother tried to stop him.'

'How do we know you're not lying?' Isabel asked. 'How do we know you weren't going to kill us?'

Thorn fixed his eyes on her. 'I could have done it in the corridor. I was right beside you in the dark, remember? Or I could have done it in the storeroom. I could have killed you anytime.'

'But you didn't.' Isabel glanced at Ash, but he was silent, still reeling from the idea that Pierce had ordered his death.

'No. Because I wanted to help you. But it doesn't matter if you don't believe me. What you *do* have to do is stop Pierce from getting off this island. If you don't, millions of people will die. Pierce thinks he's going to sell *Kronos* to The Broker – a man who wants to control it,' Thorn said, 'but he's wrong. The Broker isn't a man; it's an organization – a doomsday cult that wants to save the planet by wiping it clean and starting over. A few chosen people will be given *Zeus*, then *Kronos* will be released across the world and everything will begin anew. A simpler world.'

'They want to kill *everyone*?' Isabel whispered.

'The explosive from the storeroom,' Thorn said. 'I have some right there in my pack. Detonators and handset too. Use it to put a hole in the boat. Whatever happens, they can't leave this island. And if you're lucky, you might even be able to save your parents.'

'How?'

'There's a radio transceiver on the boat. The only way to

communicate off island. Before you use the explosives, set the radio to channel seventy-two and broadcast a coded message. Repeat it every minute until you hear a response.'

'What message?' Isabel asked.

'*Titan Down.* I have people standing by on the mainland. They can be here in well under half an hour.'

'Right.' Isabel looked at Ash, then at the painkillers in his hand. 'Give them to him. Let's go.'

Ash hesitated, then threw the box down into the hole and stood up.

'There's something else you should know,' Thorn said as they were about to walk away. 'About your dad.'

'My *dad*?' Ash stopped and looked back.

Thorn took a deep breath and rubbed a hand across his face. 'I'm sorry, Ash. What happened to him . . . When your mother refused to give Pierce what he wanted, he organized a way to persuade her. What they were going to do to you . . . they already did to your father.'

'No.' Ash felt a flush of grief and confusion. 'It was an accident. Hit and run.'

'It was murder, Ash. Your father was killed on purpose. Pierce ordered it. He wanted to—'

But Ash didn't hear the rest of what Thorn was saying. All he could think about was that car coming off the road and ploughing into Dad. It was the same thing he had seen over and over again in his head, except now it wasn't senseless and it wasn't an accident. It was a vicious murder.

And there was something else gnawing at the back of Ash's mind. A twisted thought with a terrible black heart.

What happened to Dad hadn't been his fault.

It had been Mum's.

And he was here because of her.

06 hrs and 53 mins until Shut-Down

They left the bunker in silence, emerging into the fragrance of the jungle. Howler monkeys, watching in the dark from the treetops, tensed when the door opened. They sat forward on their branches and trained their eyes on the boy who emerged. The frogs and insects continued to croak and chirrup as if everything was normal, but nothing was normal.

They struggled up the incline towards the ridge Isabel had mentioned, the torch lighting their route ahead when necessary. High in the canopy, the powerful monkeys shifted and followed, swinging from tree to tree in eerie silence.

Ash was still trying to process everything Thorn had told

them. He was filled with anger and sadness, everything whirling in a muddle of misunderstanding. 'I can't believe it. I can't believe what's happening. My dad . . . and do you think Mum *really* meant to make something so bad?'

Isabel pushed past a low hanging branch without moving it aside. 'I think adults do the stupidest things.'

Ash had thought that telling Isabel about Dad earlier had helped him to feel better, but now it was even worse. His throat was tight and his mind was awash with so many feelings. He held back his tears and made himself think of something else. 'Do you feel any better?'

'The injection?' Isabel looked back at him. 'Not yet.'

'Do you feel worse?'

'No.'

What if Thorn had been lying and Ash had injected Isabel with something else? Something even worse than *Kronos*? He shuddered at the thought of it, but all they could do was wait for it to take effect, so they walked on and on, climbing higher and higher.

With his heart heavy from the weight of everything he now knew, Ash glanced back at the monkeys from time to time, seeing them move like shadows through the treetops. He could hear their breathing, detect the beating of their hearts, and he was sure there were more of them than before. The creatures were growing in number the further they moved into the forest, keeping their distance but always watching.

When the trees began to thin and the ground levelled out, Isabel stopped and looked out across the moonlit jungle. 'We are on the ridge. The BioSphere is that way.' She pointed behind them, then turned to point ahead. 'And the bay is that way.'

'How far?'

Isabel rubbed her eyes and shrugged. 'A few hours' walk – three, maybe four? – but it is much easier up here than down there.'

Over to the right, Ash could make out the forest canopy spread below, but to the left the trees thinned out until there was just a never-ending blackness. 'And over there . . .' He sniffed the air, detecting the faintest hint of salt on the breeze. 'The sea?'

'Right,' Isabel said. 'It's close, but there are many cliffs. The bay is the only place where there is a beach.' She looked out at the world spread beneath them.

'I'm glad you're here,' Ash said. 'I could never have got this far on my own.'

'We still have a long way to go.'

After some time, Isabel shone the torch back into the trees. The light reflected from countless eyes. 'They're still following,' she said. 'They're following you.'

'I can hear them,' Ash looked up. 'I can smell them too.' It was a sweet, fruity smell, mixed with the musky smell of fur. 'But I'm not scared of them. Not any more. I don't think they want to hurt us. Actually, they' – it felt like a strange thing to say – 'kind of make me feel safe.'

'When Thorn was coming to the bunker, they warned us he was there. And he was scared of them. But I think maybe they like you.'

'How could they *not* like me?'

Isabel managed a half-smile before she reached up to pull a vine towards her. She cut through it with a clean slice from her knife and tipped back her head to let the moisture drip into her mouth.

'You look better.' Ash moved closer and focused on the sound of her heart. It wasn't so weak now – it hit every beat – and that sickly smell was becoming faint. Thorn had been telling the truth after all.

'I *feel* better.' The drips fell on Isabel's chin as she spoke. 'Not so much pain in my muscles. It really was the cure, Ash. I know it.' When she finished drinking, she held the vine out to Ash, warning him, 'Don't put your lips on it.'

Ash had expected drinking from a vine to be like turning on a tap, but it was more like turning a tap *off* and trying to catch the last few drops. He had taken less than a mouthful before he caught the scent of something unexpected on the breeze.

'I smell burning.'

Isabel sniffed the air. 'I don't smell it. Maybe it's from the bunker?' she suggested. 'From our fire?'

'No. It's closer than that.'

'You think it's *them*?'

'Yes. And I think they're close.' He scanned the forest, searching for the flicker of a fire or the winking of a light – anything that would tell him Pierce was close.

Isabel put a hand into her pocket, pulling out a disposable lighter she had taken from Thorn's pack. When she flicked the wheel, there was a spark and a small flame jumped to life. The flame leant back in the breeze, pointing in the direction they had just come from.

'Wind's coming from the north.' Isabel let the flame die, then put the lighter away and looked ahead. 'It must be carrying the smell from somewhere in front of us. OK. No talking and no torch.'

Somewhere over the sea, a bright white light flashed for an instant, then the sky rumbled long and low.

'More rain coming,' Isabel said.

They were cautious as they progressed along the ridge. Isabel tested the ground for traps or anything that might make a noise and give them away. Ash followed, stepping wherever Isabel did, just like when they had first entered the forest.

There were more flashes over the sea, and the sky continued to grumble. As he was walking, Ash tried to make sense of everything Thorn had told them. There was so much to remember, so much to digest and understand. There was *something*, though, that didn't feel right. Ash couldn't quite put his finger on it, but something was niggling at him, and the voice in his head knew what it was.

I'm keeping it to myself, the voice said. *It's a secret. You'll have to figure it out on your own.*

Ash went over it again and again, trying to remember everything Thorn had said and exactly how he had said it.

Can you really trust him? the voice whispered. *Can you really trust Thorn?*

'I can smell it now.' Isabel's voice snapped him out of his

thoughts. She had stopped and was staring along the ridge. 'Look,' she said. 'You see that?'

Ahead, maybe a hundred metres away through the trees, something flickered orange.

'Fire,' Ash said. 'It's Pierce and Cain.'

05 hrs and 26 mins until Shut-Down

'I know what you're thinking.' Isabel watched Ash staring at the orange glow dancing through the trees. The air grew cooler as the rain approached, pushing the wind ahead of it. 'But we should go past,' she said. 'This is our chance to reach the boat before them. To stop them from leaving the island. They're soldiers. They have guns. We are just kids. We have to get to the boat and call for help.'

'We agreed.' Ash didn't take his eyes off the distant fire. 'Cure first, boat second.'

'Yes, but I think they are too strong.'

'*I'm* strong. And what if this is our only chance to rescue Mum? Maybe we can get what we need and go back.'

'In five hours?' Isabel shook her head. 'It's quicker to go

to the boat and call for help, just like Thorn said.'

'Why should we trust *him*?'

'He gave me the cure. And what if we go in there and get caught? Killed? They will leave the island and everyone will die. All our friends, grandparents, uncles, aunts, everyone. The whole planet, Thorn said. We need to stop them leaving. *Kronos* can't get out.'

'But the cure is right there, Isabel. Right. *There.*' Ash pointed at the fire in the distance, feeling the frustration build. 'At least let's check it out.'

'What if they see us?'

'What if they *don't*?'

Isabel put a hand to her mouth and stared at the ground, shaking her head. 'All right. The rain will cover our sounds.'

The rain came in a hiss of white noise that blanketed the other sounds of the forest as it bore down on them. Ash stared at the campfire further along the ridge until it was lost in the downpour.

'The rain has reached them now,' he said.

'All right, check the fastenings.' Isabel touched a hand to Thorn's survival pack. 'We can't make a sound.'

Ash tightened the strap across his chest and they set off, moving to the edge of the ridge so they were just below its highest point.

Closer to the fire, Isabel stopped and scooped up a handful of mud, smearing it across her face. When she looked at Ash, all he could see was the whites of her eyes, and then the rain began to streak through the mud, like she was melting. It was perfect camouflage, so Ash did the same, wiping mud over his face and hands.

They sneaked through the trees until they neared the place where they estimated the camp to be. With the rain still pounding them, they lay down and crawled up the incline, making their way back to the top of the ridge until Ash caught sight of the fire flickering through the trees about twenty metres away.

Drawing closer to a thick clump of vegetation, they snaked beneath the wide leaves to peer out at the camp. For an adult it might have been more difficult, but neither Ash nor Isabel was very big, so they were able to get close enough to see the camp in detail.

Waterproof sheets were propped on long sticks sheltering the soldiers from the rain. Cain was perched on a log to the right of a campfire, leaning forward and eating from a mess tin. Her carbine was across her lap as if she expected to use it at any moment. Pierce was sitting on the crate Ash had seen them carrying from the BioSphere. Across his shoulder was the strap of a messenger bag that lay in his lap. The other four men – including the massive soldier he had nicknamed Hulk – were all sitting with their backs to the fire, facing into the forest in different directions with their carbines at the ready.

Ash's eyes were drawn back to Pierce who was scraping a spoon around his mess tin, finding the last remains of his meal. Ash detected the sound of movement from inside the crate he was sitting on, and was now certain it contained one of the howler monkeys. Thorn had told them Pierce was taking one off the island to provide the means to make more *Kronos*. But Ash ignored it and concentrated on Pierce. He tried to read the rogue scientist, hearing the clink of metal on metal, smelling the sweat that soaked his shirt and the sourness of his stale breath. And when he looked at the scientist's profile, he felt a rising hatred. He hated the way he licked his spoon and the way he looked. But this was more than he had expected to feel. He had an irrational sense that this was not a man but a monster, and there was a powerful urge to draw his knife and rush over to the man he had first seen at Dad's funeral. He would stick his knife into him, and—

Something touched his hand and Ash looked down to see Isabel's fingers there, stopping him from taking out his knife. He blinked hard, as if coming out of a trance, and shoved the half-drawn knife back into its sheath.

'What were you going to do?' Isabel said as soon as they moved away from the camp. She was trembling and her voice was a tight whisper. 'I thought you were going to do something stupid.'

'Pierce's bag. Did you see it? I bet that's where everything is. We need to get it. If we can distract them, we—'

'There are soldiers,' Isabel hissed. '*Soldiers!*'

'But I'm strong and quick,' Ash argued. 'I can grab Pierce's bag and—'

'*I'm* not strong and quick. Not like you. And look how they guard the forest. They will see us, and then there will be no one to stop them from taking that boat. We have to keep going and call for help. We have no choice.'

'There's always a choice. That's what Dad would say.'

'But your dad is not here.' Isabel's words cut into him.

Ash glared at her, the rain falling between them. He reached for the tag round his neck. 'There is one other choice. We split up. I go for the camp; you go for the boat.'

'*What*? No way.'

'Think about it. You're not as strong and quick as me, but you *do* know the way to the beach. You can set off now, and I'll get the bag and come after you – I can follow your trail, you know I can. I'll be so fast they won't know what hit them, then I'll catch up with you. It's the *only* way to save everyone.'

'And if they catch you?'

Ash looked in the direction of the camp and shook his head. 'They won't.'

05 hrs and 00 mins until Shut-Down

In the shadow of a large tree, Ash sharpened the tip of a long branch to make a primitive spear.

Isabel took a chunk of HEX13 from Thorn's pack and moulded it round the end of the spear. She put one of the small silver detonators into the putty and switched on the handset.

'I still think we are stronger together.' Rainwater dripped from her lips.

'I know.' Ash could see the fear in her eyes, smell burnt rubber in the air around them.

'I hope you are right about this.' She nodded at the lump of HEX13 on the end of his spear.

Ash wiped away the beads of rain that clung to his

eyelashes. 'Just remember; channel seventy-two. Titan Down.' He had to believe that if Thorn had been honest about the syringe in his pack, then he was being honest about everything else.

Isabel looked at Ash, as if she were about to say something, but then just turned her eyes to the device and bit her bottom lip. She held the handset close to the detonator and pressed the button. A pinprick of green light appeared at the tip of the detonator, and the screen illuminated Isabel's face as she selected the 'smoke' option and touched the 'confirm' button. She cleared her throat and swept the wet hair out of her face. 'It's ready.'

'OK.' Ash's stomach lurched.

'It'll be thick. Hard to breathe. You need to put something over here.' She held a hand over her mouth and nose.

Ash glanced around, then drew his knife and cut a strip from the hem of his shirt. He held it away from the cover of the tree, soaking it in the weakening downpour. 'This will have to do.' He wrung it out and tied it round his neck like a scarf.

Isabel stood and took Thorn's survival pack when Ash offered it to her. She fastened it so it was hanging by her hip. 'I'll set it off in five minutes.' She pointed at the small lump of HEX13 on the end of the spear. 'Good luck.' She came forward and gave Ash a hug. She wrapped her arms right around him and held him for a moment before breaking away. 'Five minutes.' She glanced at her watch, then turned and disappeared into the night.

Watching her go made Ash feel empty inside. They had

been a good team. Together they had managed to make it this far, but alone, things would be very different. He hoped he hadn't made a mistake.

Lying in the undergrowth, he began to count. It was the only way he had to keep track of time. He listened to the beats of his own heart, thinking each one to be a second from the other, and told himself he was Ash McCarthy. He was strong. He could do this.

It's going to fail. You'll never do it.

He tightened his jaw and banished the voice to the darkest part of his mind. He concentrated on counting. On what lay just a few metres through the trees.

Three minutes left.

Scooping up more wet dirt from the ground, he reapplied his camouflage, just to be sure, then drew his knife from its sheath and hefted it in his left hand. The spear was in his right.

Two minutes.

He glanced up at the howlers sitting in the branches. They were more tense now, as if waiting for something to happen. Even during the downpour, they had made no attempt to seek shelter, but remained at their posts, fur flattened against their bodies so the muscles rippled in their shoulders. Not one of them had followed Isabel.

Ash took one last look at them and crept forward, following the smell of the fire, inching closer to the camp.

One minute.

There it was. The fire. Orange light flickering through the trees.

He pulled the damp cloth up over his mouth and looked at the HEX13 stuck to the tip of his spear like an oversized lump of chewing gum. The tiny green light was barely visible from just a few centimetres away, but when Ash looked at it, the light clicked red and he knew that somewhere in the forest, Isabel had triggered the handset. There was a hiss like a match being struck, and the end of the makeshift spear was engulfed in a thick, white, blossoming smoke.

Now.

Ash leapt to his feet in a single powerful movement. He sprang forward like an animal, his footsteps light, his muscles strong as he sprinted through the undergrowth. He ducked overhanging branches and leapt over protruding roots. He *flowed* through the forest as if it were his natural home.

Above, the monkeys began to howl.

The swirling, pulsating, all-powerful sound rippled across the forest. A continuous wave of growling, whooping and grunting from at least fifty monkeys that was answered first by the one imprisoned inside the crate in the clearing, then by others deeper in the forest. The agitated howlers jumped from tree to tree, rattling the branches, showering leaves and bugs and fruit onto the forest floor.

It was an aggressive display but Ash felt no threat from them as he hurtled on towards the spot where he and Isabel had hidden to watch the camp. As he reached it, he spotted Cain getting to her feet, shocked by the sudden eruption in the treetops. The other soldiers were doing the same, raising their weapons, pointing them into the forest.

Ash didn't waste a second. He drew back his right arm and launched the spear as hard and high as he could. At school he had never managed to throw a javelin more than a few metres, but this one sailed up like a rocket, leaving a trail of dense white smoke. It passed between the trees as it rose higher than Ash could have hoped. And when it reached its highest point, it slowed, then tipped and began its descent.

It couldn't have been a more perfect shot. The spear landed slap bang in the middle of the camp, spewing smoke, smothering everything in a thick blanket that curled out into the surrounding vegetation like a prehistoric mist.

Immediately, the soldiers were engulfed in it and Cain began issuing instructions as it invaded their lungs, making them cough. Dark shapes stumbled about in the clouds, some of them heading towards the spot where Ash had been, but he was already moving. As soon as the spear began its descent, he shifted the knife into his other hand and broke to the right, circling the camp, racing towards the spot where Pierce was sitting.

The howlers formed a seething circle in the canopy around the clearing. They clung to the branches, shaking them, creating a storm of sound that merged with their fierce growls and whoops. They tore nuts and fruit from the trees and flung them down in a hail that disappeared into the smoke.

'Thorn?' Cain's voice lifted above the haze. 'Is that you? What the hell are—' Her sentence was cut short by a powerful attack of coughing.

Ash kept to the shadows, moving quickly.

'We had no choice, Thorn,' Cain called when she had recovered, but her voice strained against the smoke that ravaged her throat. 'You know' – she coughed – 'how these things work.'

When Ash came to the rear of the camp, he stepped into the smoke and got down on his stomach where it was less dense and easier to breathe. As soon as he was engulfed in it, disappearing from view, the howler monkeys stopped as if someone had flipped a switch. They settled in the tree-tops, becoming still, peering forward and watching in silence.

The smoke stung Ash's eyes, but the damp cloth kept the worst of it from his throat. He crawled on and on, wriggling through the plants, grazing his knees and elbows on the rockier surfaces of the ridge while Cain and her men tried to regroup and organize themselves.

'Young and Petersen go left.' Cain was still coughing. She couldn't see her men, but she issued orders, hoping they could hear her. 'Winter and Jacobs go right. Spread out. Five metres.'

'What the hell was all that noise?' someone asked. 'What *was* that?'

'Was that *monkeys*?' said another. 'Was that—?'

'Follow my orders,' Cain interrupted. 'And watch the trees.'

'Watch the trees? What the hell is going on here? Why's it gone so quiet?'

Their voices were close, their shapes moving in the white

smoke, but Ash used the light of the fire to find his bearings. The flickering glow danced and twisted in the haze, turning the forest into an alien landscape of moving shadow and light.

And there was the crate. Right in front of him. A hunching darkness, with Pierce's shape standing beside it, coughing, turning this way and that, trying to see into the fog.

Now!

Ash jumped to his feet and ran towards Pierce. He covered the distance in a fraction of a second, lowering his head at the last moment and ramming his shoulder into the scientist's lower back.

Pierce had no idea what hit him. He let out a hollow 'oof' as his breath went out of him and he was propelled through the air, raising his arms to protect himself from the fall. The palms of his hands struck the ground first and he crumpled onto his stomach. Before he had time to recover, Ash was on him, grabbing the back of his jacket and spinning him round.

He then yanked the cloth away from his mouth so Pierce could stare up into his mud-covered face.

'You!' the scientist snarled. 'You can't have it.' He wrapped his arms around his chest, gripping the bag tight. 'Help! Cain!'

Ash reached down and grabbed the strap of the messenger bag. He tugged hard enough to lift Pierce clean off the ground, but Pierce still held onto the bag, refusing to let go.

'Cain!' he shouted again. 'Get over here!'

Ash put the point of his knife against Pierce's stomach and looked the scientist in the eye. 'Let go, or I'll bleed you like a pig.'

Pierce's eyes widened. He lifted both his hands. 'All right, all right. You can have it.'

As Ash pressed the blade up against the thick strap of the messenger bag, preparing to cut it loose, there was only one thing going through his head. He was going to save Mum. He was going to save everyone.

'I don't think anyone's going to bleed like a pig tonight,' Cain said from behind him. 'Unless it's you, of course.'

04 hrs and 47 mins until Shut-Down

I told you it wouldn't work, the voice sneered. *You're useless.*

'Drop the knife,' Cain said. 'And let him go.'

Ash kept the weapon where it was and looked back through the thinning smoke to see Cain a few metres away. Her carbine was pulled tight against her shoulder, and she was aiming down the barrel at him. Ash knew he was fast, but he wasn't *that* fast. Not faster than a bullet.

He raised his eyes and glanced at the dark shapes in the treetops. The monkeys sat hunched as if ready to explode into action at any second, but they remained silent and still.

Do something! Ash willed them to move. He needed help but there was no one to give it. *Help me!* Perhaps if the monkeys would call again, they would create enough of a distraction to—

'I'll only ask one more time,' Cain said. 'Let him go.'

Ash lowered his gaze. There was no use wishing for help from the monkeys. They were just animals, after all.

He sighed and let Pierce go.

'The knife.'

Ash tossed it to one side.

'Good boy. Now get down on your knees. Put your hands behind your head and lace your fingers together.'

Ash did as he was told.

Pierce got to his feet and came forward. He put a boot against Ash's chest, intending to shove him into the dirt, but Ash grabbed his foot with both hands, twisting hard so that Pierce's whole body rotated and lost balance. Before he knew what was happening, Pierce slammed face first onto the ground. It took a second for him to recover, but as soon as he did, he scrambled over, grabbing Ash's discarded knife. Once he was on his feet, he moved around behind Ash and put his left hand on the boy's forehead, pulling it back. With his other hand, he reached around and pressed the blade against his throat. 'Useless kid. You were such a disappointment.'

As he said it, something shifted in the crate, thumping hard against the inside of the lid. Pierce whipped his head round in surprise, staring at the wooden box, but was distracted by a grunt from somewhere among the trees surrounding the clearing. He looked up in the direction it had come from, seeing the dark shapes squatting in the branches. The largest of them came forward on its perch so that its features were half-visible. Shards of moonlight glowed on the glossy black fur. The streak of grey shone like silver.

'What are you looking at?' Pierce snarled at it.

The monkey grunted once again and bared dagger-like incisors.

Pierce watched for a few seconds, a confused expression passing across his face before he turned his attention back to Ash. He threw another nervous glance at the monkey, then tightened his grip on the knife and adjusted his footing as if he were about to cut the boy's throat.

'Stop!' Cain kept her weapon raised as she came into the light. 'Put the knife down.'

Pierce ignored her and leant forward so he was speaking in Ash's ear, spittle flecking against Ash's skin. 'Do you have any idea how much trouble I've gone to over the past months? Your mother was so damn stubborn. After all the work we did together, she had me shut down and then she tried to keep this away from me. Wanted it to be her little secret. Then the helicopter, and traipsing through this godforsaken jungle. And now you think you can take it away from me? Did she send you? Did she think you could save her?'

'Pierce, put it down,' Cain repeated. 'I don't think they like it.'

'What? Who?' Pierce sounded incredulous.

'Them.' Cain tipped her head towards the monkeys perched in the trees.

'Don't be ridiculous. Why would they care what—' He stopped mid-sentence.

The other monkeys had come forward now. They loomed over the clearing, each of them baring their teeth in warning.

A confused expression fell across Pierce's face as he scanned the troop of howlers. 'What are they doing? Why would they—' He looked down at Ash, eyes widening. 'My God,' he whispered. 'They're protecting you? It must have worked. In some . . . *strange* way . . . our little secret worked. And there's something I didn't expect. A connection.'

'The rest of you, weapons down.' Cain gestured to her soldiers. 'No sudden movements. And Pierce, for God's sake will you lower your knife?'

Pierce stepped away and lowered the weapon, staring at Ash as if he were in some sort of trance. '*It worked.*'

The shock of those two simple words was like a flare lighting up inside Ash's head. He turned and stared at Pierce as the veil of confusion was finally ripped away.

It worked.

With those words, everything finally began to make sense.

Since he had woken in that white room, Ash had been wondering what was happening to him. Why he felt the way he did. Why he could do the things he could do. Why he'd had such a strong sense of having been in the bunker before. And now he was beginning to understand.

It was because he *had* been in the bunker before.

He had locked the terrible memories away, but seeing Pierce and hearing his voice was bringing them back. This was not the first time Ash had been on *Isla Negra*.

Ash stared into Pierce's eyes as he remembered . . .

The house on the cliff is the boy's favourite place on the island. With its white walls and gold-trimmed windows, it's like a castle in a storybook, overlooking the sea that twinkles in the sunlight. From the tower, he can look out and see the whole world. But now something dark and terrible dwells in that tower. 'This will be our secret,' the monster says. 'Our little secret. You can't tell anyone.' But the needle is glinting in the light from the window and it looks so sharp when the monster holds it up for the boy to see. The boy's face crumples and the tears begin to flow. 'Please, Uncle Damian, I want Mummy.' He pulls away, but the monster holds him tight and leans down to whisper in his ear. 'Do as I say, you little brat. Stop snivelling and keep still or I'll hurt you. And then I'll hurt your mummy. Is that what you want?' The boy shakes his head and bites his lip. 'Then keep your mouth shut. And remember; this is our little secret.' And then the needle comes down and disappears into his skin, and . . .

The jumbled flash of images and sounds hurtled into his mind and exploded. Ash reeled with the force of their arrival, and put his hands up to his dirty face as if he could protect himself from his own buried memories. He muddled through the shapes and hazy pictures of the building and the needle and the man, without being able to fix on anything, but when he opened his eyes and looked up, he knew exactly who he was looking at.

The man behind the voice. The monster in the dark.

Damian Pierce.

The man who had made him what he was.

Now Ash was ready to understand everything.

04 hrs and 40 mins until Shut-Down

Kneeling in the wet dirt, Ash composed himself and looked around the camp. A burning hatred for Pierce reared inside him like a flaming dragon, but he had to control it. The scientist was not important now. All that mattered was the bag he was carrying.

Three other soldiers – including Hulk – were standing close to the flames, but they weren't watching Ash; they were turning in slow circles with their eyes fixed on the shapes that moved in the canopy. The fourth soldier was missing.

'Get up.' Cain crouched beside Ash and leant close. 'On your feet.' She grabbed the piece of material round his neck and hauled him up.

In the trees, one of the monkeys grunted.

'What are they doing?' Hulk swept his weapon around in the direction the noise had come from. 'You think they're a threat? There must be more than twenty of them up there.'

'They're just monkeys.' But Cain kept one eye on them as she nudged Ash towards the centre of the camp. 'How did you get out of the BioSphere?'

Ash kept quiet and tried not to look at Pierce. He continued to cast his eyes about the camp, looking for an escape. His whole body was shaking with fear and frustration, his mind still swimming with the flood of memories.

'And what's this?' When they were close to the fire, Cain took hold of the makeshift spear that was embedded in the dirt and pulled it out with one quick tug.

The tip of the spear was still sharp where Ash had whittled it with the knife, except instead of raw wood the tip was now covered with dirt and traces of white dust. Cain sniffed at it, then touched it and rubbed the dust between finger and thumb. 'How did you make all that smoke?'

'It was Thorn. He's out there right now,' Ash said, trying to sound as cold and mean as he could. 'Probably just waiting for the right moment.' It was difficult to hide the tremor in his voice.

Cain raised her eyebrows and studied him for a moment before smiling. 'Clever boy. Keeping us on our toes.'

A light thump came from somewhere by the treeline.

'Check it out, Winter.' Cain signalled to Hulk.

Despite his size, the big man was light on his feet as he ventured closer to the trees. 'Can't see anything.' Another thump made him snap his head up and look at the water-proof shelter they had improvised. 'Maybe something—' An orange-green fruit hit the ground beside him, making him step back and scowl at the trees. 'The monkeys are throwing fruit. Can you believe that?'

Pierce clasped the messenger bag to his chest. 'We need to get away from here.'

'We can handle Thorn,' Cain told him.

'You almost couldn't handle this *child*.' A flash of anger in Pierce's eyes. 'Anyway, we've got more than just Thorn to worry about.' He nodded towards the trees. 'We need to get away from them.'

'They're just monkeys.' Cain glanced at Pierce. 'It's just fruit.'

'Nothing on this island is "just" anything,' he replied. 'Something even *I* forgot.'

Another projectile hit the ground, followed by a *pat-pat-pat* as three more missiles came from the trees in rapid succession.

'All right.' Cain threw the spear to one side and gripped her carbine with both hands. She examined the shapes lurking in the canopy and addressed the other soldiers. 'Where's Petersen?'

She had to be talking about the orange-haired soldier. He was the only one missing.

'Still out there,' replied Hulk. 'You think Thorn is out there too?'

Cain reflected for a moment, still scanning the camp, and Ash saw a shrewd intelligence behind her eyes.

'Sounds like they've stopped,' she said eventually. 'Young, go and check on Petersen. Stay sharp. Winter, you watch the perimeter. And *you*' – she looked at Ash – 'can tell me where Thorn is hiding.' Her eyes searched Ash's face, and he knew she would detect his lies. She would not be easy to fool, and she was not afraid. When he read her, there was no scent of burnt plastic hanging around Cain – just a powerful smell of oil and what he guessed was gunpowder. Her heart had the strong and slow pulse of an athlete.

'We need to go,' Pierce said again. 'Petersen can catch up.' Pierce, on the other hand *stank* of burnt plastic. But there was a tang in the air too, like electricity. He wasn't just afraid. The way his voice heightened and his pulse quickened, Ash knew he was excited. 'Forget Thorn. Just bring the boy. That's an order.'

Cain shifted her eyes and looked at Pierce standing there in his scruffy suit. 'What did you mean just now,' she asked. 'When you said "it worked"?'

'What?'

'You looked at the boy and said, "It worked".'

'Did I? What the hell does it matter?'

Ash knew why it mattered, though. He had dreamlike half-memories of Pierce injecting him, watching him, testing him. He was the worst kind of monster, because he looked like a harmless fool. A wolf in sheep's clothing who had called Ash useless when the injections showed no sign of working. But now it *was* working and *that's* why it mattered.

'We're leaving,' Pierce said, coming forward, reaching

out to take hold of Ash. 'Right now. Bring the boy with us.'

'Not yet.' Cain moved between him and Ash.

Pierce stopped and tried to stand even taller. He stared Cain right in the eye. 'I think you're forgetting who's in charge here – who's paying the bills.'

'I haven't forgotten, but you don't give the orders any more. I do. And I do not leave my people behind.'

'You left Thorn.'

'He was *your* man.' Cain's eyes narrowed, and she glared at Pierce. Her fingers tightened around her weapon. It was clear they didn't like each other; maybe Ash could make use of that. So when Cain coughed, just a small and insignificant sound, it gave Ash an idea.

'*Kronos,*' he said. 'It's not just in Mum's lab; it's all over the BioSphere. Starts like flu, makes you cough. My friend Isabel has it, and now so do you.'

'Impossible,' Pierce said. 'We've all been vaccinated against the virus. Anyway, if it escaped the lab and your friend has it, then why don't—' He glanced up at the monkeys and a vague smile passed across his lips as if he had just stumbled upon a secret.

'*You've* got it,' Ash said to Cain. 'All of you. Pierce probably injected you with *Kronos* instead of the cure. It would be a good way to get it off the island: inside you. He probably—'

'We'd be dead before we got to San Jose,' Cain said. 'No, we don't have it. The real question is, why don't *you* have it? You're telling the truth about your friend, I can see it in your eyes, but why aren't *you* sick?' She turned to

Pierce. 'And why do *you* look so smug about it?' She raised her weapon at Pierce, and the other soldiers followed suit. 'Something's going on here,' she said, 'and I want to know what it is. Are you and Thorn trying to pull some kind of trick?'

Pierce backed away, lifting his hands and shaking his head. 'There's no trick. Really, this is getting out of hand.'

'Thorn was your man.' Cain looked down the sights at Pierce. 'You insisted on bringing him along. How did he get out of the BioSphere? That place was supposed to be locked down. Did you have some kind of plan to take us out? Pick us off in the jungle and save yourself some money?'

'Of course not. We're in the jungle by accident. We were supposed to be in the bloody helicopter, miles away from here by—'

'Then tell me what's going on.' Cain's tone was cold and unyielding. 'Why isn't the boy sick? *Where is Thorn?*'

'I . . .'

'Winter, cut his throat.'

Hulk drew a large black-bladed knife and approached Pierce with purpose.

'No! Wait!' Pierce put his hands in front of him, palms out. 'I really don't know where Thorn is. *Really.* And the boy?' He looked to the trees. 'It's because of them. The monkeys. It's the same reason they don't have it.'

Cain signalled one-handed to Winter, and the huge man stopped in his tracks. He remained poised to act as soon as Cain gave another order.

'Please.' Pierce took a deep breath, his attention jumping from Winter to the knife in his hand. 'I hardly know Thorn any better than you do. He's The Broker's man.'

'*What*?' Cain couldn't hide her surprise.

'And that boy' – Pierce pointed at Ash – 'is more valuable than any virus. I thought it didn't work. I thought it was all wasted, but there he is. Can't you tell he's different?'

Different. The word stood out to Ash. It repeated over and over in his head. He really *was* different.

'What are you talking about?' Cain said.

'Back there.' Pierce moved his hand and waved it behind him. 'When he came out of the forest, he was so quick. I didn't think anything of it, but he just lifted me off the ground like I was no heavier than an overnight bag. Look at him, for God's sake, he's just a scrawny little kid. I'm eighty-five kilos, and he can't be more than thirteen years old. How many other children do you think could do that?'

Cain glanced down at the boy she had captured, re-appraising him as if she were seeing him for the first time. Ash stared back at her, feeling the strength in his muscles, preparing to accept and understand what he was.

'And you see how the monkeys watch him? And *Kronos* . . .' Pierce squinted at Ash, now unable to hide his excitement. '*Kronos* doesn't affect him because it's a part of him. It's—' Pierce waggled his fingers, searching for the right words. 'It was Type Twenty-four. I knew that was the one – that's why I tried it on myself – but I was so stupid. It had to be someone who was still developing. A child. It had to be a child.' Eyes alive with pride and self-importance, he was like an excitable boy who had been keeping a marvellous secret he was finally allowed to reveal. 'I was so angry when it didn't work. Angry with you.' He pointed right in Ash's face.

'Pierce, if you don't start making sense in the next ten seconds, I'm going to let Winter cut your throat just for the hell of it.'

'Yes. Yes. Of course.' Pierce came closer to Ash. 'But it's complicated.'

'*Un*-complicate it.'

'Type Twenty-four is a performance enhancer. From *them*.' Pierce gestured towards the night, not noticing the way the shapes shifted and the branches swayed. 'Adaptable, strong, intelligent. They have genetic markers that shouldn't be there; markers I would expect to find in other animals. Feline, serpentine, pteropine, even tardigrade – a virtually indestructible micro-animal.'

Pierce took off his glasses and wiped them on the front of his shirt. 'Someone did something on this island during the war; something way ahead of their time. The animals were genetically altered. A new kind of evolution began before BioMesa ever arrived, and it continued unchecked. Everything here became something *more*. Especially them.' He waved his hand at the treetops again. 'They are strong, intelligent, hyper-aware, with senses more usually seen in other species. Can you imagine a *human being* with those abilities? An *evolved* human. Can you even begin to imagine how this kind of science could be developed? Imagine' – he waggled his fingers again – 'having bones that could heal in days; an athlete with enhanced strength; a soldier who is unaffected by extreme temperatures, who can run for miles without ever tiring, whose eyes will never fail. I thought I had harnessed the essence of what makes them different, and I gave it to this boy many years ago, but it didn't work. He was such a disappointment, but now he's back here and something . . .' He shook his head. 'Something must have triggered it. Microbes. Something in the air, the water . . . I need to investigate further, but it explains why he slept for so long. He was changing. *Becoming*.'

'You're telling me you know this boy? You experimented on him?' Cain was trying to make sense of what Pierce was telling her. 'Did his mother know?'

'Of course not. She's too narrow-minded; she would never have agreed.'

'But she found out.' Ash allowed his hatred to rise to the surface and burn stronger. All his life he had been afraid of this man without even knowing it. His was the voice in the darkness. But Ash wasn't afraid now. Pierce was just a pot-bellied scientist in a scruffy suit, while Ash was something else. Something *enhanced*. 'She found out and she stopped you.'

'Stopped me? She *ruined* me, and took you away. But look at you now. Stronger and faster.' He turned to Cain. 'Don't you see how valuable this is? *Kronos* doesn't matter any more. We don't need this primitive beast.' He kicked the side of the crate, making the monkey inside grunt. 'Not when we have this boy. *Kronos* is child's play in comparison. This boy is priceless – the most significant scientific breakthrough since . . . *ever*. I have to know how much stronger and faster he will become. I can reproduce Type Twenty-four and—'

'Heads up.' The words came from somewhere behind him. 'It's me, Petersen. Look what I found.'

Cain whipped around. 'Where's Young?'

'Checking for others.'

Ash risked a look back and saw the orange-haired soldier called Petersen emerge from the jungle. But he was not alone. Walking in front of him, with her fingers laced together over her head, was Isabel.

'Another one?' Hulk said. 'This some kind of school trip? How many *more* kids are out there?'

'None,' Petersen replied. 'It's clear.' In his left hand he was carrying Thorn's survival pack. 'She had this.' He hefted it to Cain, who caught it one-handed and held it up for inspection. When she had looked it over, she came so close to Pierce that their noses were almost touching. She fixed him with her icy-blue eyes. 'We haven't finished. I'm coming back to you.' Then she turned to Ash and showed him the pack. 'This belongs to Thorn. Why is he helping you?'

But his mouth was dry and he couldn't speak. Isabel had been their best chance of disabling the boat and calling for help, but now that chance was gone.

'Thorn is not helping us,' Isabel answered for him. 'We took it from him.'

'Is that so?' Cain put the pack over her shoulder. 'And what else did you take from him?'

Petersen dug Isabel's handset from his pocket. 'She had this but it looks dead. I can't figure out how to turn it on.'

Cain took it from him. 'Some kind of smartphone.' She studied it for a moment, then looked at Isabel. 'What is this?'

'My phone.'

Ash focused his thoughts, trying to think of a way to overcome Cain and the others. If only he could get the monkeys to—

Isabel glanced sideways at him and looked up twice in quick succession as if she wanted him to see something.

When Ash followed her line of sight, he saw that her fingers were no longer tightly laced together behind her head. She had separated her hands and was holding three fingers out straight.

What is that? Three what? Three people?

'I've never seen a phone like this,' Cain said. 'Is this some kind of messaging device? Have you been messaging someone?'

Isabel didn't show any fear. 'No. There's no signal.'

'Are you in contact with Thorn?' Cain demanded.

'No.' Isabel lowered her head as if she was looking at the ground, but she cast a sideways glance at Ash once more and widened her eyes in warning. She drew one of the fingers back into her fist so now there were only two.

What did it mean? Two what?

'If I find out you're lying to me . . .' Cain warned.

'I'm not.'

Cain looked at the handset again, searching for a way to

switch it on. She pressed the button on top, but the screen remained blank.

'It's dead.' Isabel's expression gave nothing away.

'I've had enough of this.' Cain was losing her icy calm. 'Switch the damn thing on. Right now.'

'It's dead. I told you.' Isabel drew another finger back into her fist.

One left. It's a countdown. One minute left until what?

Cain snatched one of Isabel's arms and, for a moment, Ash thought she must have seen the signal. But then she turned Isabel's hand over and slapped the handset into it before drawing a knife from the sheath across her chest. 'Switch it on.'

Isabel stared Cain right in the eye as if she wasn't afraid of her at all. She looked at her for a few long seconds, then the handset beeped twice.

That wasn't just monkeys throwing fruit, Ash thought. *Isabel was throwing HEX13. She's rigged the camp!*

In that instant, a loud *KA-BOOM!* echoed in the jungle, accompanied by a blinding white flash.

04 hrs and 31 mins until Shut-Down

A surge of energy blasted through the camp, bringing a cloud of stinging debris. Ash reeled like a drunk, blinking hard in confusion, but the effect wasn't as intense as it had been in the BioSphere. His body had already adapted to protect itself, and by the time the second explosion split the night, he had recovered enough to see what was happening.

In the canopy, the howler monkeys had whipped into a frenzy of sound and movement. They growled and grunted, leaping from branch to branch. A shower of broken sticks and unripe fruit rained down like a storm and they bared their teeth, screaming at the men below.

Soldiers blindly fired into the forest. *Brrratatat!* Bullets found their mark, slamming into the animals, knocking them from their perches, sending the others wild. The screaming rose in pitch as they encircled the camp like an attacking army.

Still disorientated, Ash turned his attention to Pierce, standing just a few metres away. He steadied himself, then moved towards him as another detonation tore through the trees. Several monkeys were caught by the explosion, ripped from the forest and propelled into the camp. Ash stumbled in the shock wave but kept going as a series of hollow pops, like balloons bursting, came from the forest. White smoke filled the air and shapes moved in the haze as the howlers began to descend from the trees.

Brrratatat!

'STOP FIRING!' Cain ordered. 'CHECK YOUR TARGETS!'

'Get them away from me!' Pierce's voice came out of the smoke.

Ash jogged through the fog towards the voice. He was almost on Pierce now. But something else was coming too; low muscular shadows were closing in like demons.

The monkeys wouldn't harm him, though. He was sure of it. They were here to protect him. He could walk past them, take the messenger bag, and they wouldn't do a thing to hurt him. He had nothing to be afraid of. But as he took another step towards Pierce, surrounded by chaos, fingers grabbed at the back of his shirt.

Ash spun round, putting up his hands, ready to fight, but Isabel barrelled into him, yelling in his face. 'Get down!

Flashbang!'

Without time to think about it, Ash let Isabel push him towards the fallen log, shoving him into the place where the old tree met the ground. He clamped his hands over his ears as Isabel jammed herself in beside him, then a fraction of a second later a deafening *BANG!* thundered in his head and a mind-numbing, intense light flashed across the clearing.

It was as if the sun had burnt itself out right there in the camp. Even with his eyes closed and his face buried in the nook of a fallen tree, Ash's whole brain lit up. Cain and Pierce and every other living thing nearby would have been blinded by the flashbang.

Once it was over, Ash opened his eyes and got to his feet. The camp was a mess, debris scattered all over, smoke wafting in from the trees. The lid of the wooden crate was splintered, but the large howler that had tried to smash its way out had been caught in the crossfire and was slumped, half in, half out, its lifeless arms trailing on the ground. Many other monkeys – more than Ash could count – sat huddled and afraid, blinking, trying to see. They growled and bared their teeth at the slightest noise. Cain was crouched in the same place Ash had last seen her, both hands covering her eyes. Winter was on the ground, doubled up in pain, and Petersen was lying dead. Around him, the clearing was littered with the corpses of howler monkeys.

Pierce was writhing in agony, holding his hands to his face.

'Quick!' Isabel grabbed Ash's arm. 'There's another soldier out there.' Her voice sounded quiet and distant even though she was shouting.

'Stay here.' Still woozy but recovering quickly, Ash stumbled back into the camp.

Cain was kneeling now, with her head up and the stock of her rifle pulled tight against her shoulder. Her hearing was beginning to return, but Ash could tell she was still blind.

'Thorn?' she was saying. 'We didn't want to leave you in there, but there was no choice. Everything was going wrong and we had to get out.'

Some of the monkeys were coming to their senses now. They turned their heads, picking up the voices. Some leapt to their feet and stood on all fours, muscles rippling beneath their fur. They were strong and adaptive; it wouldn't be long before they were on the attack once more.

Ash moved out of Cain's line of sight and snatched up a rock, throwing it over her head to land close to Petersen's body. She spun round. 'Thorn?'

While she was facing away from him, Ash picked up Thorn's survival pack. He slung it over his shoulder and ran to Pierce, grabbing his knife from the forest floor beside him and slipping the blade under the strap of his messenger bag.

'Please.' Pierce became still and put out his hands as he looked up without seeing anything. His eyes were open, but they moved from side to side as if he were searching for something, and Ash knew the flashbang had blinded him.

'Please, Thorn. Please. We *had* to leave you.'

Cain whipped round again, her weapon pointing towards them. 'Thorn? What are you doing?'

Ash put the point of the blade against Pierce's chest, letting him feel it digging in.

'Don't do this.' The pitch of Pierce's voice heightened as his throat constricted and panic gripped him. The stink of burnt rubber flooded from every pore, mixing with the metallic smell that hung in the smoke. 'Don't kill me. Cain, don't let him kill me.'

Ash looked at his face, glad to see him so afraid. After everything Pierce had done, he deserved this. Dad was *dead* because of him. Ash began to wonder what it would be like to push the knife harder, to force it all the way through to his shrivelled heart.

'Don't,' Pierce begged. 'Thorn. *Please.*'

Ash snapped out of it and leant down to whisper in his ear. 'Type Twenty-four worked better than you thought. I'm not what you think I am, *Uncle Damian*. I'm even better.'

Pierce froze. His mind struggled to process who had just spoken and what they had just said. 'Wh . . . what?'

Ash sliced upwards, cutting through the strap and pulling the messenger bag away from Pierce.

The scientist stared at nothing, his face fixed with an expression that lay somewhere between fear and confusion. 'Better . . . ?'

Ash held the bag in his left hand, the knife in his right, and stepped away. Cain was still pointing her weapon, the barrel aimed directly at Ash, her eyes looking left and right, blinking hard as her sight returned.

Ash moved further to the side and began to walk backwards, careful not to make a sound.

'Better . . . ?' Pierce said aloud, questioning himself. He half sat up, his head turning as if he was looking for something, but his eyes still failed him. 'Better how?' His voice grew louder as Ash moved back across the camp. 'Better *how*?' Pierce scrambled onto all fours and began running his hands along the ground, searching for a weapon. 'Tell me. Stop. Stay where you are, you little brat. You think you can just walk away from me? Stay where you are.'

Ash reached the log and climbed over it, looking back at Pierce who was turning his head in desperation, crawling about, coming closer to where Petersen's body lay.

'Cain,' the scientist shouted. 'He's getting away. Stop him. Shoot him! Don't let him get away.' His hand brushed over the body and he patted along it, finding the right arm, prising the pistol from Petersen's dead fingers. Without hesitating, he raised it up and fired into the air in front of him.

CRACK!

Ash flinched, even though the pistol wasn't pointing anywhere near him.

'Where are you, you brat?' Pierce was saying. 'Where the hell are you?' The pistol kicked in his hand once more, the shot flying wide and crashing into the trees to Ash's right. He then swivelled and began firing in different directions so that bullets cracked into the forest and thumped into the ground around the clearing.

Ash jumped for the cover of the fallen tree and looked over at Pierce, firing at anything that made a sound.

Cain, on the other hand, was almost perfectly still. She was on one knee, her weapon lowered. Her vision was still hazy, but she knew she was not alone. All around her were the dark shapes of the howler monkeys. They emerged from the forest and the thinning smoke, moving along the ground on all fours, tails held high, muscles flowing beneath their fur.

'Put your weapons down.' Cain's voice was calm. 'Pierce, stop shooting.' When she unslung her weapon and placed it on the ground, some of the monkeys came forward to swat it away. They stayed close to her, pushing their faces close to hers, baring their teeth and growling.

Cain held her hands out to either side and lowered her eyes in submission. 'Don't aggravate them.'

Behind her, Winter had followed her order, and was now on his knees, surrounded by monkeys. Pierce, on the other hand, was on his feet, pistol pointed in front of him. He fired again, but it was the last time he pulled the trigger.

With a savage outburst of howling, more monkeys came forward as one, seething from the trees, heading for Pierce. A terrifying tidal wave of teeth and nails, they clawed at him, beat at him with their fists and pulled him to the ground, swarming over him like a pack of rabid wolves.

Pierce didn't even have time to scream.

04 hrs and 26 mins until Shut-Down

Ash and Isabel ran into the night as if the hounds of hell were on their heels. They didn't care how much noise they made or how the undergrowth whipped at their legs; all they had to do now was get to the boat. They were almost there. They had almost won. No one would be taking *Kronos* off the island, so the world was safe from the virus, and now Ash just had to concentrate on calling Thorn's helicopter and saving Mum.

They ran and ran, pushing deeper into the forest.

'How . . .' Isabel panted, 'are you not tired?'

'Type Twenty-four. That's what Pierce called it.' Ash was still trying to process it all. Adrenalin was firing through his system, making his mind work at a million miles per hour.

'It's the island. And something Pierce did to me when I was younger. Something to do with the monkeys.'

'I heard what he said, Ash, I was there, setting my trap, but . . . can it be real?'

'It must be. It explains everything that's happening to me. And I think the monkeys really *were* protecting me, but I don't know how much. I mean, they left Cain alone when she put her gun down, so maybe it's just guns they don't like.'

'Or maybe she was not a threat any more. But they gave us some time.' Isabel looked at her watch as they ran.

'And you. You were amazing. That was such good thinking. Why did you come back? I mean, I'm glad you did, but—'

'As soon as I left, I knew it was a mistake. And when I saw they had caught you . . . I started throwing . . . HEX13 into the forest. It was lucky I didn't blow us all up.' She gestured at the messenger bag. 'Is it all there?'

'Yeah,' Ash said. 'Looks like it. Pierce's keycard too. For the lab.'

As they continued through the forest, Ash began to recognize the first signs of dawn breaking. The sight of the reddish glow over the forest in the distance was bittersweet, though. It would be good to chase away the dark, but the rising of the sun reminded him that time was running out for Mum.

Isabel stopped and reached up to take hold of a vine. 'We need to rest for a moment.'

'We need to keep moving,' Ash said.

'I'm not like you.' Isabel took the knife from Ash's belt and sliced through the vine. 'If I don't rest and drink, I'll be in trouble. The sun will be up soon and it will get hot. Very hot. You need to drink too. There's another vine there.'

'A few minutes then, but that's all.' Ash sliced through it in one go and waited for the sweet drips to fall onto his tongue.

'*Let go or I'll bleed you like a pig?*' Isabel's mouth cracked a wry smile. 'That's what you told Pierce. I heard you when I was planting the HEX13.'

'Is that really what I said? I don't remember. I was so scared.'

'Me too,' Isabel admitted.

'We did it though, didn't we? We got away.'

'We haven't got away yet.'

Ash waited for more drops to fall into his mouth, then swallowed. 'You think Cain will come after us? You think the monkeys will let her?'

Isabel continued to hold the vine as she looked over at Ash. 'What did they do to Pierce?'

Ash stared out at the forest and let the vine water drip onto the carpet of leaves by his feet. 'You don't want to know.'

'But he's dead?'

'Definitely.' Ash felt no sympathy for the scientist. 'But maybe if Cain doesn't pick up her rifle, the monkeys will let her just walk past them. Can she follow us?'

'She doesn't need to. She knows where we are going.'

'Then we just have to move fast,' Ash told her. 'You OK to

keep going?'

Isabel nodded.

'And is there any HEX13 left?' He unfastened Thorn's pack and looked inside.

'Yes. Detonators too.'

'And you still have the handset?'

Isabel dug into her pocket and pulled it out for him to see.

'Then I say we finish this once and for all. Let's get to that boat.'

03 hrs and 46 mins until Shut-Down

They went back up to the ridge and jogged along the old path, where the jungle was thinner. To their right, the sun was rising, evaporating last night's rain and shrouding the forest in mist.

As Isabel grew tired, they slowed to a quick walk, and after a while, Ash stopped completely and listened. He closed his eyes and reached out for any further sign of pursuit. The gentle breeze in the canopy whispered with the sound of autumn leaves tumbling on the pavement. Insects creaked and birds chattered. In the undergrowth, creatures foraged. Even the trees hummed as they drew nourishment from the ground. Ash focused beyond all of those things, reaching out as far as he could until he heard a different type of movement. The regular fall of boots on dirt.

'They're coming,' he said. 'Four people. Maybe three. Running. The howlers are still in the trees. I can hear them too.'

So they picked up their pace and hurried on, trekking for almost an hour before they eventually emerged from the embrace of the forest into the full glare of the sun.

They stood, parched and red-faced, looking out at an expanse of thin and rocky dirt, where only the hardiest plants grew in ragged tufts. It stretched ahead of them to a point where it seemed to fall off the end of the world, and teetering on the edge was a large, derelict two-storey building.

'The bay is close now,' Isabel said.

Ash looked out at the end of the world. 'You think the boat's there?' he asked.

Isabel shook her head. 'It *has* to be.'

They jogged across the open ground, knowing that Cain would be close behind, and when they neared the cliff, Ash stopped. From where he was standing, a one hundred and fifty metre sheer drop fell to the bay below, where the surf broke on a large beach of shining black sand. But beneath his feet was a pot-holed road that trailed away to the right, snaking along the edge of the cliff. In the near distance, the cliff height began to drop and the road sloped down until it reached sea level at the far end of the bay. At the midpoint of the beach, a small wooden jetty extended out from the shore. Moored to the end of it was what they were hoping for. The boat.

The beach itself was empty, apart from a shabby, square concrete building with an ancient radio antenna protruding from its roof. Attached to the antenna was a thick wire that ran up to the plateau and connected to the tower of the building to the left of where they were standing. But the majestic two-storey building was a phantom of its former self. The white paint had faded and peeled from the stone, and the red-tiled roof was now a soft garden of emerald and gold moss.

The house on the cliff is the boy's favourite place on the island. With its white walls and gold-trimmed windows, it's like a castle in a storybook, overlooking the sea that twinkles in the sunlight. From the tower, he can look out and see the whole world . . .

Being close to it gave rise to a gnawing, sickening feeling in his stomach. 'I've been here before,' Ash said. 'I think this is where Pierce injected me with Type Twenty-four. I'd forgotten it, but after what Pierce said . . . and actually *being* here . . .' He stared at the building, trying to recall the distant memories of a small boy.

'Come on.' Isabel looked behind them. 'We don't have time.'

Snatched away from his thoughts, Ash turned and saw Cain and the others as clearly as if they had been only a few metres away, their faces contorted with the effort of having pushed so quickly through the jungle. It was also easy to spot the shapes of the howler monkeys in the distant trees. There were *hundreds* of them now, moving from branch to branch. And when they reached the jungle edge, they came to a halt, forming a thick line that stretched twenty metres in each direction. They settled, like an army on a battlefield, then began to howl. The sound flooded across the rocky plateau like a tidal wave: a mournful call that Ash knew was a warning to him.

01 hr and 26 mins until Shut-Down

'This way!' Isabel took off at a sprint, racing around the right side of the building. Ash followed close behind.

They passed beneath a crumbling balcony, heading towards an ornate stone railing built right onto the edge of the crag. On the other side of the railing, the cliff fell away in a sheer drop to the beach, more than a hundred metres below. It would be easy to tumble over and fall to a messy death.

They followed the railing around the building, until they came to a break in the barrier.

'Apart from the road, this is the only way down,' Isabel said.

'My God. You've got to be joking. That's *it*?'

The black steps were little more than fifteen centimetres wide, carved into the cliff face, zigzagging down to the beach. There were metal posts buried in the rock at regular intervals, with wire strung between them to form a flimsy handrail. Even when it was first built it would have been dangerous, but right now it was a death trap. Some steps were broken away while the rest were coated in slippery moss, and to make matters worse, the railings had all come loose so the wires hung limp from their securing.

Ash summoned all his courage and sidled close to the edge, but it was like looking into a void and his vision began to swim. He felt woozy, his stomach lurched. If he fell down there he would bounce off the rocks like a water-filled

(*blood-filled*)

balloon, smashing from crag to crag until he finally landed dead in the black sand. The world spun around Ash and he stumbled forward, foot slipping on loose rocks. For a second he teetered over the brink of the void, then he felt Isabel grab the back of his shirt and pull him away.

'You OK?'

Ash nodded and rubbed his face. '*No one's* getting down that way.'

'Then what do we do?' Isabel's voice rose. 'If we use the road they'll catch us. Or shoot us. I'm sorry. We shouldn't have come to the steps. I thought . . .'

Ash looked at the loose wires from the railings, then down at the beach below. The boat was *so* close. He stared at it for a moment, wishing there was some way of getting down there quickly, some way to— He jerked his head round and looked up at the tower to his left. 'There,' he said. 'Maybe there's another way.'

Ash put his shoulder to the heavy front door and pushed it open on moaning, rusted hinges. A damp smell oozed out, accompanied by a flutter of disturbed wildlife and a long, low creak from the heart of the building.

Ash hurried in, aware of the ghosts that had haunted him: the white and gold house, the monster with needle-like fangs. He had been in this place. A long time ago, when he was a different person, his feet had touched these floors. Images swam in his memory, overlaying the mansion as it was now with images of how it had been. Just being there made his stomach cramp.

But he had faced Pierce. This place held no power over him.

I am Ash McCarthy. I am strong. I can do this.

He ran across the main hallway – a huge space, with a high ceiling and a wide central staircase that split halfway up and swept around to either side of the first floor. The balustrade was flaked with peeling gold paint, and the steps were covered in carpet that was once scarlet and plush but was now threadbare and grime-coated.

Damp had eaten through the ornate ceiling so that rotten beams and plaster hung from holes like the building was spilling its guts. The walls were a mess of peeling wallpaper and huge patches of mould, and the corners of the room were thick with bird droppings.

'We need to get to the tower.' Ash started up the stairs, wondering if maybe this was a bad idea, but they only had a few more minutes before Cain caught up with them.

At the top of the stairs, the landing stretched in both directions, with windows all along the front giving an awesome view of the bay. The glass in every window was smashed, and plants forced their way through, bursting like green explosions along the wall.

Dodging the broken floorboards, they sprinted along the landing and came to a door hanging crooked from its hinges. Beyond it was a narrow flight of stairs.

'I think this goes to the tower,' Ash said as they climbed. 'I remember it.'

'*Madre de Dios*, it stinks,' Isabel complained.

'Imagine how I feel.' The stench of decay was overpowering and Ash put a hand over his mouth and nose, concentrating on pushing it away. The air stung his throat and lungs and made his eyes stream with tears, but he kept going until he came to the top and pushed through a door into a huge square room with a giant bed against the far wall.

There were still sheets on the bed, but they were tattered and covered in a dense layer of filth. One leg had been gnawed right through by animals, so the bed was at a crooked angle, and the floor around it was thick with droppings and rubbish collected by birds to build their nests.

Three massive arched windows lined each side of the room

'Look!' Isabel ran to the window at the front of the building and pointed at the figures heading across the scrub towards them. 'They're getting closer.'

'Get away from the window. Don't let them see you.' Ash hurried to the opposite side of the room, but when he looked out at the sea a sudden tidal wave of dreamlike memory crashed over him.

He faltered under the weight of terrifying images, and he was suddenly a toddler again, pressed close to the open window with Pierce's hand on the back of his neck.

They have come up to the tower to watch the storm over the sea. Each time lightning flashes, the boy shudders. Thunder follows, drowning the sound of the waves crashing on the black beach. It is dark inside the tower and Uncle Damian takes the boy to the window. A spark of lightning gleams on the needle as it goes into his skin, and when it is over, Uncle Damian lifts him and holds him close to the open window so he can look down at the churning sea. 'This is our secret,' he says with a soft grin. 'You can't tell anyone. Not even your mother. If she finds out, I'll bring her up here and make her fly from this window. You think she can fly? Imagine what would happen to her if she couldn't. See how far it is to fall? You don't want that, do you?' When the scientist releases him, the boy looks up and his eyes fix on the badge on the scientist's jacket. The boy is old enough to know the letters on the logo, but too young to form the words. BioMesa. But instead of an 'O' there is a black sun with eight points radiating from it. To the boy, though, it doesn't look like a sun.

To him, it is a spider.

'So what now?'

'Hmm?' Ash shook the memory away.

'What now?' Isabel looked at the wire Ash had taken from the railings by the cliff. He had gathered a length of it and twisted it into a coil that he now held in his right hand. 'Is that for what I think?' she said.

'Yes. It is.' Inside, he was a wreck, but he tried to sound brave. He was overwhelmed by memories of what had happened here, and petrified by what he was going to do next, but he really couldn't see any other way.

Other than surrender, this was the only choice they had.

01 hr and 10 mins until Shut-Down

Ash unlatched the broken window and shoved it open. His stomach cramped when he leant out and turned round to look up, but he told himself he was strong. He could do this. It was Pierce who had made him afraid, but now Pierce was gone.

About half a metre above his head, a large metal plate was bolted to the wall, with a thick taut steel cable protruding from it. Ash reached up and tugged it hard to test its weight.

'You're crazy,' Isabel said. 'You can't use that.'

'It'll be like a giant zip-wire.' Ash turned and scanned along the cable, seeing where it stretched over the balcony, past the cliff with the rickety steps and out across the bay.

It continued at an angle, running all the way down to the concrete building on the beach below. 'I'm not heavy, so it should hold me.'

'Like the river crossing? No, it's too dangerous. Stay here, and—'

'And what?' he asked. 'As soon as Cain gets here, she's going to kill us and take this bag.' He patted the messenger bag he was carrying across his chest. 'And she's going to leave in that boat. There's no choice here. No. Choice. I mean, if you can think of any other way,' Ash said, 'please tell me now. Anything.'

Isabel took a deep breath and shook her head. 'I don't have anything.'

Ash blinked hard. He felt as if he was floating somewhere above his body, looking down on a crazy boy about to do a crazy thing.

'Once I've called for help, I'll use the last of the HEX13 to damage the boat.'

'You remember the channel number and the message?' Isabel asked

'Seventy-two,' Ash heard himself say. 'Titan Down.'

'Right.'

With his heart stuttering, Ash took a bandage from the survival pack and split it in half, winding the pieces around his small hands for protection. He touched the identity tag and muttered the McCarthy mantra, then unravelled the wire he had brought from outside. He wrapped it tight around one hand and leant out of the window to throw the loose end over the steel cord that ran down to the beach. After wrapping it tight around his other hand, he lifted his feet off the floor to test the strength of the cable.

'Don't forget . . .' His voice trembled. 'Try to break the cable once I'm down. They mustn't follow me.'

Ash stepped up onto the window ledge and sat down, looking out over the endless drop beyond. The breeze whisked about him, chilling the sweat that had broken out all over his body. He couldn't feel his legs any more. All he could feel was the hammering beat of his heart.

He tugged once more on the wire to check it would take his weight, then tried to shuffle further forwards on the window ledge, but his body didn't want to work.

'*Buena suerte,*' Isabel said. 'Good luck. And . . . thank you.' She paused. 'For doing this.'

'*De nada,*' Ash mumbled, and tried to make himself drop, but couldn't. His muscles were frozen in fear. 'Isabel?'

'*¿Sí?*'

'I need you to push me.'

'Are you sure?'

'Push me!' He shouted the words, forcing strength into himself, making himself angry and determined and unafraid. 'Push me!'

He felt Isabel's hands on his back.

'*Buena suerte,*' she said again, and gave him a good, hard shove.

There was a moment of weightlessness, then a sudden jolt as the wire became taut. It dug into his palms, tightened in the places where it was wrapped around the back of his hands, and cut off the blood supply to his fingers. But Ash didn't notice any of that. All he could think about was falling.

Falling and dying.

01 hr and 05 mins until Shut-Down

The wind lifted his shirt and snatched at his hair as he zipped out over the endless chasm.

The fear of it grabbed Ash like the devil had thrust a hand through his chest to take hold of his heart and squeeze. No breath would enter him. No sound could escape him. All he could do was force every last drop of strength into his fingers and grip the wire like his fists were made from the hardest granite.

He couldn't let go. Whatever happened, he could
NOT
LET
GO.

His eyes watered as he stared at the drop below his

dangling feet. The black cliffs sped away behind him, and then he was hurtling more than a hundred metres over the rocky beach with only the strength in his hands to keep him alive.

Tears streamed away from the corners of his eyes.

I am strong. I can do this.

He repeated the words over and over in his head as he gathered speed. The cable hummed above him, the wire whizzing along it, rasping like a giant zip unfastening. The wind howled in his ears and pummelled him as he started to swing from side to side.

Despite his strength, his hands were burning. The pain was excruciating, and when something jarred him hard the wire tugged tighter, biting into his hands. It threatened to cut through the bandages and slice into his skin like cheese wire. Ash opened his mouth and howled as another bump made the wire dig deeper, slipping further. It was uncoiling from around his fist like a snake, trying to slice through the skin as it went.

He looked up at the wire to see what was jolting him, but the speed and height made his head reel and he had to fight to stop himself being overcome by dizziness. He was moving so quickly it was impossible to fix on anything above him, so he looked ahead, seeing the kinks in the cable. And then he hit a pair of them, two in close succession, making the wire rip further from his fists. Ash yelled out in pain and fear. Too many more and he would lose his grip. Too many more and he would fall to his death.

But he was moving like a bullet, already past the cliffs

and out over the water, rocketing towards the concrete bunker that was sunk into the gleaming black sand. If he hit the roof at this speed, he probably wouldn't survive anyway. The impact of hitting the concrete would be immediate and deadly. Ash had to release before he reached it. He had to let go when he was still over the sea.

And then the world dropped into delicious slow motion as his heightened reactions kicked in. The air no longer screamed in his ears, but hummed a low and tuneful melody. The wind caressed his face and he felt the treacle-like motion of the wire slipping thought his fists. Below him the shimmering sea moved with a dreamy slowness, while above him the wire zipped along the cable without haste. He could see and prepare for every approaching crimp, and he could look below to focus on choosing the best and safest place to drop.

There?

Just a little further.

The cable purred and the wire rippled.

'NOW!' He shouted the word as loud as he could, the sound tearing from his throat, but his hands refused to let go. The world resumed its normal pace with a rush and a pop, and once again Ash was hurtling to his death, his fists locked tight, as if they were fused to the wire.

'Let go!' Still they clung to the wire. 'Let go! Now!'

He let out a long, loud yell and focused everything into his hands, forcing his fingers open so that the wire skidded through them, slick with blood and sweat.

Then he was falling, momentum carrying him forwards as

he dropped.

'Yes!' he shouted as his narrow frame crashed into the waves and cut deep into the sea.

The salt water bubbled and foamed around him, catching him in its tow, but as soon as his feet touched down, Ash pushed hard and shot to the surface. He broke through the waves and gasped for breath, treading water as he wiped his eyes and looked back at the tower. Isabel was there, standing in the window, so he raised a hand to her and she waved back. As he watched, though, a shadow appeared behind her.

Isabel's hand dropped and she whipped round, but she was too late. Arms came out of the shadows and grabbed her, pulling her into the darkness of the room. In an instant Isabel was gone, and Ash watched in horror as Cain's face came into the dark rectangle and looked down at the sea.

Acting on instinct, he took a breath and ducked beneath the waves, turning and swimming as fast as he could. His mind was filled with the awful things that Cain would do to Isabel, terrible images flashing through his thoughts as he swam to the small jetty he had seen from above. And when he reached it, he stopped beside one of the wooden struts until his breath ran out, then rose slowly to the surface and looked back.

The window was just a dark rectangle once more, and the clifftop was clear.

01 hr and 04 mins until Shut-Down

On this side, there was no obvious way to board the boat from the water, and the jetty was too high to reach. Ash swam around to the stern, where the name '*Olympian*' was painted in bold black letters, and spotted a low swimming platform. He pulled himself onto the boat, throwing the messenger bag and survival pack onto the deck beside him, and lay face down with his cheek against the wet fibreglass.

He was terrified for Isabel. He had no idea what Cain would do to her, but had seen enough to know that it wouldn't be good. All those bodies in the BioSphere, the blood . . . He had to put it out of his mind. All he could do was find the radio and use Thorn's distress call. Hope that

Cain would keep Isabel alive for a while longer.

'Come on,' he told himself between breaths. 'Keep moving.'

He struggled to his feet, weighed down by wet clothes, grabbed the bags and climbed over the stern to drop into the boat. He crossed the deck and peered through a glass door into the cabin and galley. Plush cream leather seats were fixed in an 'L' shape to Ash's left. Beyond them were the wooden worktops of the galley and a set of steps descending deeper into the boat.

The *Olympian* swayed with the motion of the sea, groaning and creaking as Ash scanned for evidence of a radio. Seeing nothing, he stepped back and noticed a ladder heading to the level above. Ash rattled up the ladder and found himself on the bridge where a pair of leather seats were bolted to the floor in front of an array of controls. In the centre of the panel was what looked like a radio.

Ash went straight to it and pulled the handset away from the dash. He put it to his mouth and pressed the button on one side. 'Hello?'

Nothing. Not even a hiss of static.

'Hello?' he said again, keeping the button held in as he studied the main radio unit. There was a digital display on it, but it was dead – just like all the other screens on the dashboard.

'Power,' Ash muttered. 'How do you—' He spotted the ignition, close to his knees, with the key still in it. A metal 'O' hung from the key ring, swinging gently from side to side.

Ash took hold of it and closed his eyes.

'Please work.'

When he turned the key, the engine stuttered and jumped into life. He had not expected it to work first time, so he was filled with a surging sense of victory. He was now one step closer. Soon, this would all be out of his hands and he could let someone else take control.

The screens and dials lit up and the radio let out a long, sharp hiss.

Pshshshshshshshsh.

'Yes!' Ash reached across to the main unit and pressed the channel button repeatedly, his fingers shaking, blood running from the cuts on his palms.

When the readout finally displayed a large 72, he tried the handset once more.

'Hello?'

Pshshshshshshshsh.

His heart began to sink. Thorn had been lying.

'Please.' He held the button down again. 'Please. Titan Down. There has to be someone there. Please.'

Pshshshshshshshsh.

Click. 'Er . . . say again. Over.'

The voice made Ash jump and a burst of excitement shot through him. 'I said, Titan Down. Titan Down.'

Pshshshshshshshsh.

Nothing.

Ash pressed the button again. 'Titan Down. Did you hear me? Please. Titan Down.'

Click. 'Reading you five. Loud and clear. Titan Down. Please stand by.'

There was a long pause filled with static and Ash looked up towards the clifftop, seeing no movement. The window in the tower was still just a dark rectangle. 'Anyone there?' he said, pressing the button on the handset once more. 'Titan Down. Titan Down.' He kept his eyes on the clifftop, wondering where Cain was now. 'Titan Down. Titan Down.'

Click. 'You can stop saying that now.'

He froze.

'Sit tight. I'm on my way.' Thorn's calm voice was unmistakeable.

Ash tore his eyes from the clifftop and stared at the handset. How on earth could Thorn reply to his radio message? Wasn't he supposed to be stuck in a dark hole in a bunker in the middle of the jungle?

'We'll be there in five minutes,' Thorn said.

Ash watched the handset as if it might hold some answers to his questions, but he caught movement out of the corner of his eye and looked up to see Cain and her men jogging along the road by the mansion.

Isabel was with them, surrounded so she couldn't escape.

'Hurry.' Ash spoke into the handset. 'They're coming. I have *Kronos* and *Zeus.*'

'Just stay calm,' Thorn replied. 'I'll be there in five and we'll get off this godforsaken island.'

'After we help my mum.'

Pshshshshshshsh.

'I said, "after we help my mum".'

'Yes,' came the reply. 'Of course, after that.'

On the clifftop, Cain and the soldiers were waving their arms as they ran, as if to attract his attention. They were forcing Isabel to do the same, trying to trick him.

Ash scanned in front of them, seeing how far they would have to travel before making it down to the beach. Five minutes, he guessed. That should be enough. Thorn would be here by then. But it bothered Ash that Thorn was on the other end of the radio.

He pressed the button and spoke into the radio handset. 'Thorn?'

'Right here.'

'Are you in a helicopter?'

'Affirmative.'

'How?'

Pshshshshshshshsh. The static hissed into the quiet morning before Thorn came back on. 'I have a locator and health monitor implanted under my skin. I hadn't moved for a long time, and my vital signs had dropped, so my people thought I was in trouble. They got worried and came look-ing for me. It's all good, Ash, it means they got here quicker.'

This *was* good news. It meant that help was already here and they could fly straight to the BioSphere to save Mum. Everything was going to be OK.

But for some reason it felt wrong.

Ash watched the figures running along the clifftop and remembered what Thorn had told him about how Dad had died and about how he was here to stop Pierce and Cain from getting their hands on *Kronos*.

And then it struck him.

It was so obvious. How had he not realized before?

If Thorn had wanted to stop Pierce and his team from getting *Kronos*, why had he allowed them to bring everyone to the island? Hadn't Mum already destroyed *Kronos*? Why give her the opportunity to recreate it? And why had Thorn sounded so cagey on the radio just now when Ash mentioned rescuing Mum?

There were just too many questions, and trying to unravel them all made Ash's brain hurt, but something told him not to trust Thorn. There was only *one* thing he could know for certain: people were prepared to do anything to get their hands on *Kronos*. And that meant he had to be prepared to do anything to stop them.

He had to accept that he was alone, and that no one was coming to help.

54 mins until Shut-Down

Cain and the others were halfway down the cliff road when Ash heard the rhythmic thudding of the helicopter.

Thucka-thucka-thucka.

The radio crackled into life and Thorn's calm voice slid out over bridge. 'Almost there, Ash. Sit tight.'

Ash was cross-legged on the deck, with the messenger bag and the survival pack open. The contents, including Pierce's keycard, were spread out in front of him.

Two silver canisters, like thermos flasks, stood side by side, with the tops removed. Inside each one was a pull-up rack containing four slim injection guns filled with clear liquid. Four were labelled '*Kronos*' and four were labelled

'*Zeus*'. There was also a flash drive inside each canister, presumably containing Mum's notes detailing how to create the virus and its cure. Once closed, the canisters would be sealed tight, totally shockproof and water resistant.

As he arranged the contents of each bag and repacked them, Ash kept looking up to the cliff road and then to the sky as the sound of the helicopter grew closer and closer.

Tears were rolling down his cheeks because he knew he couldn't save Mum. He had done everything he could to help her and the others trapped in the lab, but he felt certain now that the helicopter wasn't coming to help them. Everything he had done was for nothing. Mum and the others would die. And in a few minutes Cain and Thorn would be here, then he too would die.

All he could do now was fulfil Mum's wish. Destroy *Kronos*.

I told you, the voice sneered. *I told you you're useless.*

The helicopter thundered over the clifftop. It flew out across the sea, then slowed and turned before coming back towards the boat. Ash watched it hovering a hundred metres away as it descended towards the waves, rippling the water in the rotor's downdraught. When it had dropped to a height almost level with the upper deck of the boat, the helicopter dipped its nose and moved forward, coming to a halt just a few metres from the *Olympian*.

'I said we wouldn't be long.' Thorn's voice crackled from the radio. 'You did well.'

Ash could just about make out the pilot through the cockpit glass, though the sun reflected from it and shone in his face. He stood and put up a hand to protect himself from the rush of whirling air, then glanced back at the cliff road to see Cain and the others nearing the bottom.

The helicopter rotated to the left so it was sideways on to the boat, and the door drew back to reveal the inside of the aircraft, complete with a mounted mini-gun. A man Ash didn't recognize threw out a rope ladder, then disappeared from view. When he returned to the door, Thorn was with him, one arm over his shoulder. His leg was encased in a white mesh cast. In his left hand he held the radio that he now put to his mouth.

'You need to come aboard,' Thorn shouted into his mouthpiece. 'You have the materials Pierce took, right? Swim to the ladder and we'll get you out of here.'

'I want to know what's going on. Who are you? Did *you* kill my dad?' Ash had to know it wasn't his fault. That it wasn't *Mum's* fault. 'Who are you?'

'I already told you.'

Ash shook his head. 'I don't believe you. I want the truth.'

'We haven't got time for this,' Thorn said. 'Swim out to the ladder.'

'The truth!' Ash shouted. He was afraid and frustrated. This wasn't the way he wanted this to happen. Thorn was supposed to tell him everything – give Ash a reason to trust or distrust him, to make some sense of what was happening.

Thorn moved the radio from his mouth and spoke to the man who was supporting him. The man nodded and helped Thorn to sit down, then moved away and took up position behind the mounted mini-gun. He swung it round to point towards the cliff road and fired a single quick burst.

The pounding shots thundered over the sound of the helicopter, and empty cartridges spilt from the weapon. They fell to the sea like sparkling, metal rain. Ash whipped around to see Cain and the others come to a sudden halt and drop to the ground.

The mini-gun fired again, kicking up dirt just a few metres from Isabel.

'Come aboard and I'll let your friend live,' Thorn said into the radio. 'Maybe I could use a kid like you.'

Ash shook his head again. Thorn had just confirmed everything. He wasn't there to help. Ash couldn't trust him.

'Fair enough. Then I just want *Kronos* and *Zeus*. Nothing else.'

Ash put a protective hand on the messenger bag that hung at his side. He took a step back and Thorn leant over, yelling to the pilot. The helicopter swung closer so the rotors were spinning not far from the top of the boat.

Thorn was just a few metres from Ash now, their eyes almost level. He nodded to the mini-gunner, who fired another burst in Isabel's direction, then he lifted the radio once more.

'I do not have the *time* for this. Throw the bag up here and we'll call it a day.'

Ash looked down at the bag, drawing Thorn's attention.

'That's it. All you have to do is throw it onto the helicopter, then all this will be over. Don't make me come and get it.'

Ash grabbed the strap and pulled the bag over his head.

'I'm losing my patience. Throw the bag to me now or I'll kill you and everyone else. And the first thing I'll do when I leave here is find every single one of your friends and relatives and kill them too. Is that what you want?'

Ash gripped the bag tight in his right hand and drew back his arm.

'That's it. Throw it, goddamnit! Throw it now!'

Ash had no other choice. Whoever Thorn was, Ash had seen the bodies in the BioSphere – he had seen what Thorn had done to those guards, and he had heard what Pierce said about him.

(*He'll gut us.*)

Ash realized he had been right to be afraid of Thorn, and knew he couldn't trust anything he said – except for his promise to kill Isabel. Ash had heard the truth in Thorn's voice when he had said *that*.

So he threw it. He hefted the messenger bag as hard as he could towards the helicopter's door so that it sailed right past Thorn and disappeared into the darkness of the interior.

Almost immediately, Thorn signalled to the pilot and the helicopter began to move away from the boat, gaining height.

The machine-gunner remained in position but took his eye off his targets as he watched Thorn turn and shuffle into the aircraft to retrieve the bag.

'Thorn?' Ash spoke into the radio.

'What is it?'

'You'll never take *Kronos* off this island.'

'What? What are you talking abou—?'

But Ash didn't wait to hear anything else. Instead, he whirled around and grabbed the HEX13 handset from the dashboard behind him. The heavy white dot tracing the letter 'Z' was still ghosting across the screen. Ash put a finger to it and copied the symbol as fast as he could.

Inside the helicopter cabin, the last of the HEX13 ignited in a searing ball of orange flame and black smoke that flashed outwards through the door, propelling the burning mini-gunner into the sea. The aircraft began to move backwards, jerking left then right with no one to control it. The pilot was screaming, his hair and clothes on fire, and when the helicopter's tail struck the water, the whole thing tipped and began drifting towards the boat, blades coming at Ash like a vicious murder weapon.

Whup-whup-whup.

Ash grabbed Thorn's survival pack and slipped it over his head as he ran to the steps and jumped to the deck below. He dived over the gunwale onto the jetty, hitting the dry boards in a roll, and then he was on his feet again, sprinting towards the beach.

Behind him there was an awesome crunch as the blades made contact with the rear of the boat. They sheared off, spinning over Ash's head and clattering onto the far end of the jetty, close to the sand. There was a squealing of metal on metal as the helicopter slammed down onto the stern of the boat, then the two vehicles erupted in a blast of flame and thick grey-black smoke.

Ash was lifted off his feet and blown from the jetty

towards the swirling sea. He flipped around, falling backwards, smashing hard into the waves. Something sharp and metal flashed towards him in the blink of an eye. He had just enough time to register that it was there before it slashed across his forehead, cutting right to the bone as it sliced through his eyebrow and down into his cheek. Pain seared through his face as water rushed around him and he sank under the waves. Eyes open, he stared at the cloud of blood billowing from his wounds.

He sank down and down. Deeper and deeper.

The world began to darken. There was no sound.

Ash's lungs collapsed as he disappeared, and then he saw something rushing towards him. Something large falling from above, smashing into the water and sinking, pushing him deeper, pinning him to the seabed.

43 mins until Shut-Down

'Ash?' The voice was coming to him from another world. 'Ash?'

Everything burnt beneath his closed eyelids. His whole body felt as if it were on fire.

'Is he . . . *Madre de Dios*.' It was Isabel's voice. Dull and distant.

Ash was in so much pain he wanted nothing more than to just fade away. The idea of dying didn't frighten him as much as he thought it would. It would be far better than living with the agony he now felt.

Just lie down and die, the voice whispered. *You know you want to.*

But there was still something he had to do. There was

- 274 -

still something he had to say, so he focused, trying to remember what he had done. He'd had a plan. He had to say something before Cain killed him. He had to—

Ash's eyes jerked open and he saw Cain leaning over him. Water was pouring off her onto the black sand. Isabel was kneeling beside her.

'*Kronos* . . .' His throat burnt when he spoke. 'Is . . . gone.' Each word was like a mouthful of crushed glass. 'Explosion.'

'That doesn't matter,' Cain said. 'What you did was very brave.'

Ash stared at her, trying to take a breath. He couldn't understand why she was being nice to him. Had *Cain* pulled him out of the water? 'My . . . pack.'

'Don't try to talk.' Cain's voice pounded in his head. 'Help is coming.'

Help? Why wasn't she trying to kill him?

'Pack,' he insisted.

'It's right here.' Cain put her hand on Thorn's survival pack still secure across Ash's chest.

'Pierce's keycard,' Ash said. 'And *Zeus*. In the canister. For Mum.'

An unexpected expression flooded across Cain's face. Was that relief? Ash couldn't make sense of it. He had beaten Cain; she should be angry.

'You kept it?' Cain said. 'You kept *Zeus*? That's . . .' She shook her head in disbelief as she opened the pack and removed the metal canister containing the injection guns.

'The flash drive . . . too,' Ash told her. 'But not *Kronos*. I blew that up. If you want . . . *more*, you have to . . . save Mum. And the others. They will have to . . . make it for you. Get to Mum. Now.'

'Jesus, you're a smart kid. A pain in the neck, but *smart*.' Cain looked behind her. 'I wish these klutzes were as brave and clever as you. With men like you, I could do anything.'

Brave? Clever? She wasn't making sense. But it didn't matter any more; he had carried out his plan.

Destroy *Kronos*. Save *Zeus*.

'Save Mum,' Ash said.

'We will.' Cain leant closer. 'Because saving the world isn't enough for you, is it?'

Ash took one last look at Isabel, then closed his eyes.

His job was done.

Death was a bright, shining light that reached into every corner and chased away every shadow. It was filled with the rhythm of breath and the beat of hearts and the scent of all the things that were most important. The familiar and comfortable smell of Mum, the sweetness of coconut, cinnamon and ginger.

'He moved.'

'Isabel?' The word escaped his lips in a single breath.

'Ash. You're awake.'

He opened his eyes. He was in a room exactly like the one he had woken in yesterday morning. Seeing the white ceiling brought back everything that had happened. The lockdown, the jungle, the clifftop mansion, the terrible explosion . . .

'Mum?' He tried to raise his head but it felt too heavy for his neck. Everything ached.

'I'm here,' Mum said. 'I'm right here. We gave you some painkillers and something to sedate you for a while, so you might feel groggy.'

'How long?' Ash let his head fall back onto the pillow and turned to see her sitting by the bed. Isabel was standing just behind her.

'A few hours.' Mum reached across to press a button and there was a mechanical whirring as the top half of the bed started to lift, pushing Ash into a semi-upright position.

He looked at Mum, seeing that her eyes were still blood-shot and her shoulders still hunched. She was tired and weak, but she was right there in front of him and he knew that time must have run out by now. Was he too late? He couldn't smell that sickening sweetness of overripe fruit on the turn, but was she dying? Had Shut-Down begun?

'You're alive,' he said.

'Thanks to you.' Mum glanced away, then forced a smile. 'Cain said you were very brave. They got here just in time. We're going to be all right. All of us.'

'You saved everyone,' Isabel said. '*Everyone.* Your mama. My papa. You were amazing.'

The relief was intense, but something cut through it. One name. 'Cain.' Just saying it made him shiver. 'Where is . . . ?'

'Right here.' Cain stepped into view and stood next to Mum, back straight, arms by her sides. She had a pistol holstered on her hip.

Ash pushed back in the bed. His instinct was to get away

from her, and he felt hatred rise in his throat.

'It's all right.' Mum said. 'She's not here to hurt us.'

Ash stared at Cain.

'We tried to tell you.' Isabel came forward. 'We were waving from the cliff. Cain was trying to help us. She works for the British government, and—'

'No. That's what Thorn said about himself, and we should never have believed him.'

'But Cain had a satellite phone. She'd already called for help. She pulled you out of the water,' Isabel said. 'She brought help and came straight back to the BioSphere.'

'Only so they can have *Kronos*,' Ash said.

'No.' Mum shifted in her seat. 'You destroyed it. Cain told me you blew it up.'

'And you didn't make any more?'

Mum shook her head.

'But she tried to kill you,' Ash said. 'She locked you in the lab with—'

'Pierce did that,' Mum told him.

'She's lying.' Ash stared at Cain. 'You knew Mum would die. And I saw you shoot down that helicopter. You were going to let Pierce kill me.'

Cain cleared her throat. 'I had to do some regrettable things – as I have *often* had to do in my profession – but my mission here was to identify a highly dangerous organization known as The Broker. Our intelligence was that Pierce was going to sell *Kronos* to The Broker. He needed a team to help him get it, so my organization put me and my men undercover and placed me close to him. He hired us and I was to follow *Kronos* at all costs. Once Pierce locked that lab and took the virus, I had no choice other than to stay with him.'

Ash read her for evidence that she was lying. A twitch or a blink. A missed heartbeat. Anything.

'It's true.' Isabel came closer and sat on the bed. 'Cain saved your mama and my papa.'

'No,' Cain said. 'Ash did that when he stopped Thorn getting his hands on that research. Until Pierce let it slip at the camp, I had no idea Thorn was working for The Broker. I can only guess that they let Pierce hire us, instead of using their own people, to avoid any link to The Broker – and to let Pierce feel like he was in charge. Pierce *liked* to be in charge, and if Thorn had chosen a team of his own, Pierce would never have trusted them. I suspect Thorn planned to pay us off as soon as we got to the mainland, let us leave, then kill Pierce and take *Kronos* to his boss. Getting trapped in the BioSphere complicated his plans.'

'And we helped him get out,' Isabel explained. 'That's why he didn't hurt us. He was using us to escape.'

'Looks like he had a helicopter waiting,' Cain said, 'just like ours was. Thorn must have been one of the few people who are close to The Broker leadership. If I had known sooner, I might have been able to get him to talk . . .' She shook her head. 'Well, the link's gone now. But don't be mistaken; that's the *only* reason I brought help. Not to save you. The Broker was my priority. With Thorn and Pierce dead, though, I had no reason to continue my mission.'

Ash watched his mum and wondered how she felt about

all this. None of it would have happened if she hadn't created *Kronos*. He wondered if she knew that Dad would still be alive if not for her work.

'Your life is going to be very different from now on,' Cain said. 'In my experience, The Broker gets what it wants, one way or another. They know who you are, so you'll have to disappear. Very few places will be safe for you. We need to leave immediately; we've already stayed longer than we should.' She watched him for a moment. 'And you're in debt. To me.'

Ash didn't understand.

'If it hadn't been for you, Pierce would be leading me to The Broker right now. You owe me.' Cain's expression was serious. 'And I think you might become very useful.'

'No,' Mum said. 'He doesn't owe you anything. You can't make him—'

'I'm afraid you don't have a choice, Dr McCarthy. There is nowhere for you to go – you belong to us now. Your son is special and we intend to find out just how deep that goes.' Cain lifted a mirror from the bedside table and held it up for Ash to look into. 'When I pulled you from the water, you were burnt and half your face was hanging off. Bringing you here in the helicopter, I watched you heal. Never seen anything like it.'

Ash looked at his green-eyed reflection and traced a finger along the cut running across his eyebrow and down his cheek. It was red and raw, but in a few more days the only trace of it would be a nick in his left eyebrow where the hair would never grow.

'We're going to find out exactly what Type Twenty-four did to you,' Cain said. 'Now, get up. It's time to leave. The pilot is already preparing the helicopter.' She turned on her heels and left the room.

Isabel bustled out after her, and the room fell into silence.

Ash put down the mirror and looked at Mum. Everything over the past twenty-four hours had led to this moment. Everything he had been through had been to protect her, and it didn't matter what she had done. He didn't care that she had made *Kronos*. All that mattered was that he had kept his promise to save her. He hadn't lost her the way he had lost Dad.

'You're so brave.' Tears welled in his mum's eyes as she reached out to take his hand. 'I'm so sorry about everything; that I let Pierce . . . do that to you. I should never have brought you to the island . . . I shouldn't have . . .' Tears were rolling down her cheeks now. 'I should never have left you alone with Pierce. I didn't know what kind of man he was, that he could do such a—'

'It's all right.' Ash took his hand from Mum's and picked up the identity tag that lay nestled in the coils of its leather cord. He put it over his head. 'Pierce changed me. This *island* changed me. It made me better.' He sat forward and put his arms around Mum. 'And I came back, didn't I?'

'Yes you did.' Mum hugged him tight.

'And I saved you.'

'Dad would be so proud.'

'I saved you,' Ash said again. 'Just like I promised.'

1 hr and 23 mins later

SOMEWHERE OFF THE WEST COAST OF COSTA RICA

The Blackhawk helicopter skimmed thirty metres above the waves as it flew out across the Pacific Ocean towards *Isla Negra*. Modifications to its design meant that it was one of a kind. The engines ran quieter than any known helicopter, and it was equipped with stealth technology and terrain-following radar to enable low-level flying. It was undetectable – a ghost that was able to deliver swift and violent destruction from its Hydra rocket pods, Hellfire missiles and dual mini-guns.

Inside the cockpit, the co-pilot watched the screen in the centre of the instrument array, then looked up at the white-crested sea. 'Continue on this heading.' He spoke into his headset without looking at the pilot. 'We'll reach in one minute.'

'Copy that.' The pilot took the helicopter lower and glanced at the screen. It showed an image of the area they were flying over, with the north tip of *Isla Negra* just visible. A kilometre from the shore, in the expanse of the Pacific Ocean, a single green dot pulsed silently. At the bottom of the screen was displayed the heartbeat, blood pressure, respiratory rate, body temperature and blood sugar levels of the owner of the green dot.

'Coming up on it now.' The co-pilot spoke once more. 'Twenty seconds.' He watched the screen. 'And . . . mark.'

The pilot slowed the helicopter and settled it into a quiet hover, descending close to the surface of the water. When he had reached the lowest safe height, he spoke into his headset. 'Ready for pick-up?'

'On your order,' came the reply from the rear cabin of the helicopter.

'Execute.'

In the rear cabin, one soldier drew back the door while another stepped forward and out. Harnessed and attached to a winch, he dropped quickly to the surface of the water where a slender man floated, clinging to a piece of wreckage from a boat named *Olympian*. His clothing was torn and singed, his hair was completely burnt away, and one side of his face was scorched and bleeding.

The soldier clipped the slender man to his own harness and spoke into his headset. 'Bring us up.'

Once aboard the Blackhawk, a medic was standing by with a syringe in one hand. He had been monitoring the slender man's vital signs and already knew what emergency treatment would keep him alive.

Exactly thirty seconds after receiving an injection, Lathan Thorn opened his left eye and took a deep breath. His whole body was wracked with pain. The leg was bad, but his face was worse. When he had been blown out of the helicopter by the HEX13 explosion, the blast had almost melted the right side of his face, sealing his right eye shut.

He looked up at the medic, then at the soldiers sitting on either side of the rear cabin. Four men to his left, four to his right, each of them armed with an FN SCAR Mk 17 assault rifle.

'Orders?' A face came into view, leaning over.

Lathan Thorn watched the team leader for a moment, but when he tried to speak, only the left side of his mouth would open. He took a moment to compose himself, then tried again. 'BioSphere,' he said. 'Centre of the island. All survivors . . . to be taken alive.'

'Copy that.' The team leader relayed the information to the pilot, and the helicopter began heading south.

Flying at over two hundred knots, it only took the Blackhawk a matter of minutes to cover the distance that Ash and Isabel had covered in hours. When the BioSphere was in sight, the pilot slowed and descended into the clearing, close to the wreck of another, less impressive helicopter.

Before it had touched the ground, the doors were open and the soldiers were jumping down, moving into formation as they approached and entered the building. Two stayed on board, stationed at the mini-guns.

Lathan Thorn remained on board too, unable to move, but at least the pain was beginning to subside.

'The painkillers will work for a while,' the medic told him. 'But we need to get you back ASAP. The longer we wait, the less we can do.'

'Keep waiting.'

'Yes, sir.'

Eleven minutes after entering the BioSphere, the team of elite soldiers returned, weapons held at ease.

'It's empty, sir.' The team leader reported his findings. 'Four security guards, who've been dead at least a day. A scientist.'

'No women?'

'No one else.'

'Children?'

'No one, sir. Not a soul. The place is a ghost ship. There's nothing here.'

Lathan Thorn closed his good eye, and for the first time in years he felt rage. Pulse-racing, thought-scrambling rage. In a lifetime of service to The Broker, he had never failed. *Never.* And he would not begin now.

This was not over. He would survive his injuries, he would heal, and then he would find Ash McCarthy. There was nowhere on earth the boy would be able hide from him.

'Orders, sir?' the team leader asked.

Thorn opened his eye and looked at him. 'Take me home. I have a job to finish.'

Acknowledgements

Writing a novel can be an adventure in its own right. There are some moments when the waters are calm, and the jungle is quiet. But other times, the jungle closes in, and the river rises, racing through rocky canyons, cascading over treacherous waterfalls. At times like those, every adventurer needs someone to throw them a rope or offer them a hand, so I'd like to take a moment to acknowledge the special people who accompanied Ash and me on this adventure.

I want to say a huge thank you to the brilliant Barry Cunningham for his advice and support, and for really loving stories. I feel proud to be a Chicken House author. Thanks to Rachel Leyshon who spent so much time patiently listening to my crazy ideas for Isla Negra, offered the right advice, and steered me in the right direction. Also to Rachel Hickman and Elinor Bagenal for so much hard work in making the book look fantastic and sending it out into the world. Thanks to my agent Carolyn for her honesty and guidance, to Bella for her priceless editorial support, and to Laura (for her patience!), Jazz, Kesia, Sarah and Esther for being awesome back at Chicken House HQ.

And, of course, I couldn't embark on any adventure in Danworld without the lifeline of my first readers – my wife, my daughter and my son. Without them, I would have washed over that waterfall a long time ago.

And you. The reader. I want to thank you for losing yourself in my world.

ALSO BY DAN SMITH

BIG GAME by DAN SMITH

Armed only with a bow and arrow, thirteen-year-old Oskari reluctantly sets out into the freezing wilderness of his Finnish homeland as part of an ancient trial of manhood. But instead of finding animals to hunt, he stumbles on an escape pod from a burning aeroplane: Air Force One.

Terrorists have shot down the President of the United States, and they're on their way to capture him. Even if the boy and the world's most powerful man can evade them, how can they possibly survive in the wild?

'Everything about this book is excellent. The story is fast-paced, extremely well written and is packed with unrelenting action.'
BOOK TRUST

Paperback, ISBN 978-1-909489-94-3, £6.99 • ebook, ISBN 978-1-909489-95-0, £6.99

ALSO BY DAN SMITH

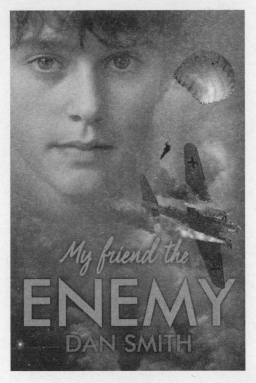

MY FRIEND THE ENEMY by DAN SMITH

1941. It's wartime and when a German plane crashes in flames near Peter's home, he rushes over hoping to find something exciting to keep.

But what he finds instead is an injured young airman. He needs help, but can either of them trust the enemy?

'. . . an exciting, thought-provoking book.'
THE BOOKSELLER

Paperback, ISBN 978-1-908435-81-1, £6.99 • ebook, ISBN 978-1-909489-06-6, £6.99

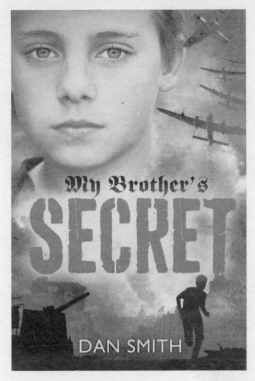

MY BROTHER'S SECRET by DAN SMITH

Twelve-year-old Karl is a good German boy. He wants his country to win the war – after all, his father has gone away to fight. But when tragedy strikes and his older brother Stefan gets into trouble, he begins to lose his faith in Hitler. Before long, he's caught up in a deadly rebellion.

'Rich in detail, this is a thought-provoking story.'
JULIA ECCLESHARE

Paperback, ISBN 978-1-909489-03-5, £6.99 • ebook, ISBN 978-1-909489-54-7, £6.99